I0636063

Florine and Boca
Tales of Faerie

Florine and Boca
Tales of Faerie

by
Françoise Le Marchand

Translated, annotated and introduced by
Brian Stableford

A Black Coat Press Book

English adaptation and introduction Copyright © 2018 by Brian Stableford.
Cover illustration Copyright © 2018 illustration by Mike Hoffman.

Visit our website at www.blackcoatpress.com

ISBN 978-1-61227-810-0. First Printing. November 2018. Published by Black Coat Press, an imprint of Hollywood Comics.com, LLC, P.O. Box 17270, Encino, CA 91416. All rights reserved. Except for review purposes, no part of this book may be reproduced or transmitted in any form or by any means, electronic or mechanical, including photocopying, recording, or by any information storage and retrieval system, without permission in writing from the publisher. The stories and characters depicted in this novel are entirely fictional. Printed in the United States of America.

TABLE OF CONTENTS

Introduction

Florine, ou la Belle Italienne was initially published anonymously in Paris in 1713 by Claude Jombert, one of the very rare *contes de fées* to be granted a royal privilege for publication after 1699. It was reprinted as the first story in Volume One of an eight-volume collection of *contes de fées* entitled *Le Cabinet de Fées*, compiled by Estienne Roger and ostensibly published in Amsterdam in 1717, but probably printed illegally in Paris. The latter version is lavishly illustrated; photographs of the illustrations—the captions of which allow the story they accompany to be identified—are now reproduced on line. The set was reprinted in 1731 and again in 1762, the latter version as *Les Contes de Fées*, with an extra volume and different illustrations, allegedly in Nuremberg. The stories are attributed to Madame d'Aulnoy and often listed in bibliographies under her name, although her works only occupies volumes three to six of the original eight volumes.[1]

---

[1] The other three stories in volume 1 are by the Comtesse de Murat, as are the first two in vol.2; the third item in volume 2 is by Mademoiselle L'Héritier and the remaining two by Jean de Préchac. The stories in the seventh and eighth volumes include works subsequently attributed, a trifle dubiously, to the Chevalier de Mailly, and the stories from *La Tyranie des fées détruite* and *Les Chevaliers errans* (both tr. in the Black Coat Press collection *The Tyranny of the Fays Abolished and Other Stories* by Comtesse D.L.) by a writer who subsequently became known in France by the entirely fictitious name of "Madame d'Auneuil," whose name presumably originated as a

"Boca, ou La Vertu récompensée" was originally published in the exceedingly scarce collection *Nouveaux contes de fées allégoriques* in 1735, also issued anonymously and illicitly, before being plagiarized in an edition printed by Nicolas Duchene, bearing the false signature "Madame Husson" and a false place of publication (London) in 1756, two years after the death of the actual author, Françoise Le Marchand, née Duché de Vancy. *Florine* and "Boca"—if, in fact, the former is really her work—are the only two works of that kind that the author is known to have published, although she is known to have written others.

Apart from the author's death date, the Bibliothèque Nationale catalogue gives no data relating to Madame Le Marchand, and information in other recoverable sources is slight, but it is known that she was the daughter of the playwright Joseph-François Duché de Vancy (1668-1704), a gentleman of Louis XIV's household, who was the king's *valet de chambre* for a time. He was a notable playwright and composer whose works—admired by Madame de Maintenon, who obtained a pension for him—were mostly based in Classical and scriptural sources; he was also an antiquarian elected as a Member of the Académie des inscriptions et médailles. His daughter is reported by some sources to have assisted him in his work, but that seems unlikely, in view of the fact that she must still have been in her teens, at the latest, when he died. She might, however have completed some of the works he left unfinished at his death, and certainly wrote plays herself, although none appear to have been published. She is recorded in several sources

---

misspelling of "Aunoi"—a version of the name of Baron d'Aulnoy, employed before its orthographical titivation.

as the hostess of a notable artistic salon attended by celebrated artists, including Charles-Antoine Coypel—who is credited with a posthumously-published *conte de fées*—and presumably by composers and writers as well.

In that regard, Joseph de La Porte, in the fourth volume of his *Histoire des femmes célèbres dans la littérature française* reports that Madame Le Marchand "was in society with many intelligent people" and that she left behind several works in manuscript that she had read to her friends, asking them to maintain an "inviolable secrecy" in their regard. La Porte gives her husband's full name as Monsieur Le Marchand de la Méry, and says that he was the *receveur-général* [tax-collector] of the domains and woods of the region of Soissons. He also states that she was the person who arranged the publication of *Nouveaux contes de fées allégoriques.*

If Françoise Duché de Vancy was acquainted with any of the authors of the first wave of *contes de fées* published in 1696-99 it can only have been as a young child, but it is not implausible that she might have been among the original audience of the fraction of those tales specifically designed for narration to children. As to how *Florine* obtained a royal privilege for publication in 1713, when they were so rarely granted, we can only guess, but Françoise Duché de Vancy certainly had influential friends at court. Even though the 1735 collection is presently unobtainable, the Bibliothèque Nationale catalogue entry does list the authors contained therein. All one-time courtiers of considerable status, they include the late Marquise de Caylus (1673-1729), who was brought up by Madame de Maintenon, the dominant female force in the court, and whose memoirs of the court were subsequently edited by Voltaire.

9

As to how Madame de Caylus's posthumous contribution came to be included in the collection, we can only speculate, but the likeliest source is her son, Philippe, Comte de Caylus (1692-1765), who might well have known Françoise Duché de Vancy as a child, and almost certainly knew her as an adult because, as an antiquarian and important pioneer of archeology, he would have been interested in her father's work. Whether he attended her salon is a matter for speculation, but it seems highly likely, if only because he refers in one of his own stories to the tale by Coypel, which had not published at the time, and which he could only have heard read aloud. His likely acquaintance with Madame Le Marchand might have been one of the factors involved in the Comte de Caylus becoming a significant writer of *contes de fées* himself.

Further light on Madame Le Marchand's salon is cast by a footnote added by Charles Mayer to the reprint of Coypel's story in the 1786 *Cabinet des fées*, with reference to Coypel's brief introduction into the story of a character named Thémire, said to be still active in Parisian literary circles. The note includes an excerpt from a letter written by Coypel to an unnamed friend in which the artist waxes lyrical about "Thémire," making it clear that it was a nickname adopted by Le Marchand:

"The moderns say, then, that Thémire is the image of their Deshoulières? For myself I say that, by the grace of God, Thémire only resembles Thémire. Thémire has an imagination so prodigious that it requires nothing less than her prodigious reason to regulate it. Now, Mademoiselle Sapho had a great deal of imagination, but reason...zeft! Madame Deshoulières perhaps had a great deal of reason, but would she have imagined *Boca*? I ask you. You can see that I'm right to tell you that Thémire only resembles Thémire. Besides which, Thémire is incomparable for sentiments. On great occasions Thémire's reason would be capable of loving the persons that her heart detested, and her mind arranges all that so well that the devil, or what is worse, a woman, could not tell whether it is the heart or the reason that loves. Finally, to complete the portrait of Thémire, her character is so mild that in all the petty bickering of society, she makes efforts to persuade herself that the wrong is on her side, and it is always the reason that dominates."

The likening of Le Marchand to "Mademoiselle Sapho" is significant; "Sapho" was the nickname Mademoiselle de Scudéry adopted in her own salon, where the writing of *contes de fées* was probably pioneered by her protégée Mademoiselle de L'Héritier, who also wrote a spectacular feminist eulogy to the poet Antoinette Deshoulières (1638-1694). The link strongly suggests therefore, that Le Marchand saw her own salon as a direct descendant of Mademoiselle de Scudéry's, formed in its image. It also makes clear that although Le Marchand published very little, she was greatly admired by at least some of the members of her salon. In Coypel's story, "Thémire" is not only credited with the "recently published" *Boca*, but also the "soon-to-be published" *Javotte*—which never actually appeared—and numerous other *contes de fées*, some of them written when she was very young, perhaps including *Florine*. Evidently, the author gave up seeking publication after financing the publication of the 1735 collection, content thereafter with the adulation of a select audience.

The self-selection of her pseudonym is also significant. Thémire is the chaste heroine of a prose narrative by the historian and political philosopher Baron de Montesquieu (although he denied authorship of it for a long time and it pretends to be a translation from ancient Greek), *Le Temple de Gnide* (c.1724). Montesquieu's Thémire is a favored devotee of a uniquely delicate cult of Venus in which the kind of amour the goddess favors is opposed to and contrasted with vulgar physical lust (closely akin to the alternative Amour featured in Madame d'Aulnoy's story "Le Pigeon et la colombe," tr. as "The Pigeon and the Dove"). Montesquieu's work enjoyed a brief heyday of celebrity, which led to Thémire being the subject of numerous songs and other literary works written in the mid-eighteenth century. As to whether Montesquieu ever attended Madame Le Marchand's salon, we can only guess, but Caylus was certainly acquainted with him, and Montesquieu would have been interested in Joseph-François Duché de Vancy's work for the same reason as Caylus.

During the six years that separated the publication of "Boca" from the publication (similarly anonymous and illicit) of Caylus' first collection of *contes de fées* a number of other significant novellas of a related stripe were published in the same fashion, including *Funestine* (1737) by Pierre-François de Beauchamps. *Tecserion* (1737) by Mademoiselle de Lubert and "La Belle et la bête" (1740) by Madame de Villeneuve. Again, there is no way of knowing, now, whether any of those writers attended Madame Le Marchand's salon, although Beauchamps was certainly acquainted with Caylus, but if one or more of them did, they might well have been key participants an intriguing community of interest. At any rate, Madame le Marchand certainly deserves to be reckoned a significant, if slightly shadowy, figure in the revival of *contes de fées* in the 1730s and 1740s.

It is not obvious, on the basis of a superficial examination of the texts, why either of the two novellas translated in the present volume had to be published illicitly, but it undoubtedly reflects the fact that the entire genre was effectively under a royal ban, save for a handful of exceptions, in the aftermath of the scandal that had caused Louis XIV's police to break up the coterie of female writers who pioneered it, two of its key members, Mademoiselle de La Force and the Comtesse de Murat, having been imprisoned and Baronne d'Aulnoy finding it politic to leave Paris in fear of arrest. Françoise Le Marchand could not have been unaware of the fact that the scandal in question involved allegations of lesbianism—unproven, of course, neither La Force nor Murat ever being formally charged with or convicted of anything, but simply imprisoned by royal edict. The latter observation might well be of no relevance whatsoever to the two works in the present volume, but the two stories each contain odd features, which might not be unconnected with that context.

In the eccentrically allegorical *Florine*, the heroine, in quest of the "imperial rose without thorns," which, we are told explicitly, is a symbol of virtue, is warned that in the course of her journey, she will meet a series of tempters who will endeavor with various degrees of cunning to draw her away from the true path to virtue and draw her to her doom. She avoids falling prey to the temptation of indolence, albeit only just, refuses even to set foot on the road to the palace of "volupté" and runs away in frank horror at her first glimpse of drunken debauchery, but yet again she only narrowly avoids the last in the sequence of temptations: marriage. What an amazing inclusion that is in a list compiled before 1717 of things to be avoided at all costs on the road to virtue, and estimated as a species of doom! Madame Le Marchand was married herself, of course—although she might not have been when she wrote *Florine*, which is easily conceivable as the work of a precocious adolescent—and *Florine* cannot ultimately escape the formularistic ending of all *contes de fées* (although it is arguable that marriage to a prince who is—paradoxically—the son of a fay does not count as an instance of conventional marriage) but that only makes the puzzle odder.

"Boca" has the same formularistic ending, but only after the prince has spent the greater part of the narrative disguised as a girl, in which guise the heroine falls in love with "her," protesting all the while that she will also love the best friend with whom she has sent many happy hours alone in "the palace of pleasure" for as long as she lives, while loathing irredeemably for the same duration the prince she has been scheduled from birth to marry. Even though the story is subtitled "virtue rewarded" it is not at all obvious that the eponymous character, who serves an agent of a benevolent fay in saving the enchanted heroine, obtains any reward at all for his trouble, and he certainly appears to live and die a virgin. What such oddities might signify is, of course, anyone's guess, but the very fact that they disrupt the conventional pattern of fantastic fictions in such strange fashions makes it difficult to regard them as mere accidents.

"Boca" is by far the more accomplished of the two stories, and it is not surprising that it was reprinted several times in the course of the eighteenth century—albeit once as stolen gods—although *Florine* was also reprinted with it in Charles Mayer's vastly-expanded *Cabinet des Fées* as well as having been reprinted in the reprints of the earlier collection. If *Florine* was, indeed, written while the author was still in her teens, that might help to account for some of the logical inconsistencies in the plot as well as its eccentric construction. "Boca" is not entirely without difficulties in those regards, but it is a far more mature work, considerably more robust and inventive in its imaginative imagery. *Florine* is certainly not without interest, however, especially in the first part, where its allegorical pretentions are more coherent and better organized. In juxtaposition, the two novellas make an intriguing pair, and an interesting example of work from a period in which very few new *contes dc fées* were allowed to reach print, in spite of the great continuing popularity of those that had been granted royal prerogatives prior to the deliberate suppression of the genre.

The translations of both stories were made from the version of volume XVIII of the *Nouveau Cabinet de fées* (reprinting material from volumes 18 and 19 of the original set) reproduced on the Bibliothèque Nationale's *gallica* website, which is the photographically-reproduced reprint edition published in 1978 by Slatkine. *Florine* was previously translated into English as "Florina" in a three-volume collection of *Novels and Tales of the Fairies* "written by that celebrated Wit of France the Countess d'Anois," first published in 1728 and reprinted several times.

Brian Stableford

FLORINE; or THE ITALIAN BEAUTY

by Françoise Le Marchand

THE PUBLISHER TO THE READER

Everyone knows that the story of a singular event renders the mind attentive and throws the soul into admiration; on young people, most of all, it makes an extraordinary mental impression and engraves traces so profound in their tender minds that they often can only be destroyed by the destruction of the body. One takes advantage of this when one wants to instruct youth, and it is the goal proposed by our author in the composition of this work. He shows us the road to virtue and felicity, when it seems that he is only talking to us about the bagatelles that make the subject matter of a tale of fays, and draws, so to speak strength from our weaknesses in rendering useful that which appears purely agreeable. It was in much the same way that Aesop instructed in his fables and the author of *Les Aventures de Télémaque* has given us excellent precepts.[2]

---

[2] The author of *Les Aventures de Télémaque*, François Fénélon (1651-1715), was the tutor of the Duc de Bourgogne, the son of the Dauphin, from 1689-97, and in addition to the cited prose epic he wrote numerous fables and apologues, in four of

Because the adventures the author describes are mostly allegorical, he has been obliged to give the individuals of which he speaks names that express their character. This is what the names signify:

Achakie   Innocence
Agatonphise   Good sense
Agnoïse   Ignorance
Amelite   Relaxation
Antadise   Obstinacy
Cliarote   Warmth
Coyphite   Recklessness
Diagine   Resolution
Dicayosine   Justification
Ergonide   Labor
Exapente   Fraud
Feliciane   Felicity
Grilison   Murmur
Hallitie   Truth
Homotille   Cruelty
Hypomone   Patience
Hypopsite   Suspicion
Leucotisse   Candor
Ociosine   Indolence
Probus   Probity

---

which he employed fays as agents of enchantment, evidently having borrowed them from the female salon writers. *Télémaque* was initially published anonymously and obscurely in 1699 but did not make much impact until it was reissued posthumously in 1717, after the death of Louis XIV, who had construed it—correctly—as an philosophical attack on absolute monarchy, hated it, and banished Fénélon from the court at approximately the same time as the persecution of the female writers of *contes de fées* began. The fables were published shortly thereafter.

Philaphtique   Self-esteem
Pisonide   Fidelity
Philopone   Industry
Psiphismate   Good advice
Ponirge   Cunning
Prelidose   Prejudice
Prodire   Treason
Photonose   Envy
Rationtine   Reason
Simpliciane   Simplicity
Sycophante   Calumny
Yssatie   Constancy
Zelopie   Jealousy
Zelopside   False zeal

PART ONE

In Italy, before the birth of Romulus, there was a prince who made the delights of his subjects. Under his conduct they enjoyed a perfect tranquility, and his neighbors, fearing his valor, did not dare trouble that mild felicity.

The prince traveled continually through all the provinces of his estates to see whether justice was being rendered exactly there. On arriving at a castle at one of the extremities of his kingdom, the queen, his wife, who always went with him, gave birth successfully to a princess who was named Florine, and who made it known as soon as she was born that she would one day be one of the most beautiful women in the world.

Scarcely had they begun to savor the pleasures of that birth than the king was told that an ambitious prince, desirous of profiting from his remoteness, had invaded his estates. That obliged him to depart with his court and all the troops accompanying him. Before that departure he summoned a sage magician in order to render the castle inaccessible to all surprises and insults, for the conservation of the princess, who remained there.

Obedient to the king's orders, the enchanter performed evocations, traced characters, invoked the powers of the air and made sacrifices to them. With his wand he marked a circle around the habitation, putting it under the guard and protection of intelligences. He buried pieces of metal and precious stones there, on which talismans were engraved. After that ceremony, although the castle was open, it was impossible to enter it or leave it without the consent of those who were there, by order of the king.

The castle was situated in the most beautiful region of Italy. It was built in marble and porphyry, and was regarded as a masterpiece of antiquity. Its enclosures responded to that, with rich compartments of a surprising beauty in which everything was found, further augmented by the enchanter's cares.

Florine stayed in the castle under the conduct of a governess worthy to bring her up and to be her example, with several women to serve her. They each excelled particularly in one of the arts that are appropriate to a young princess. They found in Florine, as she grew, all the dispositions worthy to respond to their cares. Every day Florine gave them surprising evidence of it; nothing approached the vivacity of her mind, her questions and her responses.

At seventeen, the rumor of her perfections spread. Mauritianne, one of the princesses of the fays, was curious to see whether what was said about her was true; that obliged her to quit her court and disguise herself as a simple person, and to go to the castle where Florine was. Having arrived there, she obtained permission to enter and to see the princess.

Mauritianne was surprised to see that Florine was even more admirable than her published renown, and was constrained to admit that, although she was a very old fay, she had never seen anything as charming as that princess. Mauritianne was not one of those fays who protect virtue, but one of those who are ambitious and vindictive, and make use of everything to arrive at the objective of their evil designs. It was by that means that she had risen to the rank of princess and regent of the fays, which she held, by virtue of an unfortunate adventure that had befallen Feliciane, their veritable queen.

The sight of Florine ignited an extreme jealousy in Mauritianne's heart. She formed the design of abducting her in order to doom her, but, being forewarned that her art was useless in that place as long as Florine did not go beyond the bounds of the castle, she sought a means of gaining the governess and introducing herself into the proximity of the princess, pretending to be useful to teach her embroidery work like the samples she showed them, which were imperceptibly woven.

The sage governess refused, not wanting to put a person near the princess who was unknown to her. Mauritianne was obliged to withdraw and seek other means of succeeding in her design. She thought that the emotions of compassion and generosity the princess had by nature for the unfortunate might produce the effect that she proposed.

Mauritianne remained in the vicinity of the castle, and one day, she saw the princess walking on one of the terraces of the wall. She adopted the form of an old woman, lamenting like someone overwhelmed by dolor. Having heard her, the princess sent a maidservant to see what it might be. The servant reported that it was an old woman lying on the ground, who seemed to be very poorly and who was asking for help. The princess ran there.

Seeing Florine outside the enclosure, Mauritianne seized her with one hand, and traced a mysterious circle around her with the other. Instantly, they were enveloped by a dense cloud, which hid them from the maidservant's eyes. Then Mauritianne took her away in an ebony chariot drawn by vultures, which, passing rapidly through the air, returned to her palace.

When she arrived, all the fays came to welcome her and pay their court to her. She descended from her chariot with Florine, who gave birth to contrary sentiments in the hearts of the fays. The good ones found her lovable and felt compassion for her, whereas those of Mauritianne's party could only look at Florine with angry eyes, and waited impatiently for the moment to torment her.

Mauritianne had the princess taken to one of the apartments of her palace, in order to consider what was to be done with her and the manner in which she was to be treated. Fortunately for her, that order was given to one of the good fays, who took her by the hand graciously, led her through superb apartments and conducted her to a place where the furniture was inestimably valuable.

Having sat her down in an armchair, the fay sat next to her and did what she could to help her get over her astonishment.

"Alas," said the princess, with a great sigh, "why have I been taken away from the pleasant abode where I was living tranquilly? What crime have I committed, to be removed like this and brought to a place that, agreeable as it seems, only makes me expect cruel pains?"

"The queen's jealousy of you is the cause of your abduction," the fay said. "She is in a humor to treat you badly if the good fays here do not oppose it and prevent her from taking her passion and resentment as far as she would wish. We know you and will not suffer that a person who has only ever done good should be treated as a criminal. I have felt sensible effects of that myself, and it would be the ultimate in ingratitude if I failed to give you all the help I can."

"How have I had the advantage of obliging a person like you?" said the princess.

"You will understand that," said the fay, "when you know who we are and our origin. Each of the stars that you see shining in the firmament has an intelligence that governs it. Those intelligences are omnipotent and entirely spiritual, and the influences that emanate from the stars only emerge in order to carry out their orders. Those intelligences have under their domination a large number of spirits that guide those influences in the atmosphere, in order that they are not distributed at random and that they are united intimately with the subjects for which they are destined.

"We are those spirits, and it is under our conduct that the influences are distributed. We have no bodies, and those we render visible are of a nature so pure that they ought to be taken for spirit rather than substance; we affect human form rather than any other because it is the most perfect. Our power is considerable; we dispose of the elements and all that they contain, and the perfect knowledge we have of them enables us to do things that humans take for prodigies because they are unaware of their veritable cause. As we are all knowledgeable in regard to the secrets of nature, we make use of them to do good or evil as we please.[3]

"We are not all benevolent; we retain the influences of the stars from which we emerge, which are good or

---

[3] This account of the nature of fays differs markedly from the one assumed by the *contes de fées* produced by the original coterie of writers; it seems inconsistent with the motifs that the author has borrowed from those writers—especially the physical vulnerability associated with an obligatory periodic metamorphosis, previously employed by the Comtesse de Murat in "Anguillette"—and with the fact that Mauritianne has a seemingly-substantial son.

evil, the good ones being given to recompense virtue and the evil ones to punish vice. We are not here forever; when each of us has passed the time on the earth prescribed to her, we return to the star from which we emerged, which causes some philosophers to say that we die, but that is not true; our death will only occur in the entire revolution of the universe.

"All these advantages are balanced. One day a week we are all changed differently, into a wolf, a snake, a bat or whatever animal pleases destiny, and if we receive mortal blows in that form, we really do die, without ever returning to our stars. One day, when I was a weasel, one of your maidservants was about to kill me. You forbade her to strike me. She obeyed you and I escaped, a favor for which I shall be grateful as long as I am a fay."

As she finished speaking the fay embraced the princess, who was overjoyed to receive such a salutary consolation for an action that had seemed to her so trivial

The fay took out a golden rod that she had under her robe, with which she struck the parquet where they were, and a table appeared magnificently laden with beautiful fruits, which she presented to Florine. "They're excellent," she told her, "and you need them; you haven't taken any refreshments since leaving your palace."

The princess could not dispense with taking some; she ate them and found them extraordinarily good. Then the fay tapped the parquet again with her rod, and the table disappeared.

"It's necessary," said the fay, "To hide our amity from the others as much as we can, in order that I have more facility to serve you." Then she made the princess a present of a phial of immortal eau-de-vie. "Keep that carefully," she said. "It will be very useful to you; that liquid has the property of changing all poisons into the purest substance, and however much is taken from it, the phial will always be full. That's the first help I can give you; other penalties to which anyone wants to subject you will furnish me with further means to testify my gratitude to you."

Mauritianne assembled her council, to which all the fays belonged, and addressed them.

"The person you have seen descending from my chariot is a princess whose reputation is so great that mortals believe her to be a divinity; that rumor, having reached me, excited my curiosity. I went to see the princess and it appeared to me that she had all the noble external features that are rare in persons of the world. In order to discover whether what attracts the great honors rendered to her down here, which only belong to the fays, comes from the good usage she makes of the precious gifts with which the authors of nature have enriched her, or from impulses of ambition and vanity that are inexcusable, I judged it appropriate to abduct her and to subject her to proofs that can reveal the truth."

The fays who were of the humor and the party of Mauritianne approved her sentiments and proposed to the assembly the most difficult trials, as if they were light and easy to do. But one of the fays, who had always been one of the principal counselors of Feliciane, the veritable queen, told them that Florine appeared very modest in all her actions and only had a passion for doing good; that the action of charity that was the cause of her being in the power of the queen revealed the impulses of her soul and that the lightest trials ought to suffice to convince them of it.

Having remarked that that argument appeared judicious to the assembly, Mauritianne thought that another, repeated with similar force, would overturn her designs. She said that order to avoid the tedium that speeches might cause, it was necessary to draws lots, and by that means, everyone could judge what it was appropriate to do. That advice was followed, lots were drawn, and poor Florine was condemned to spin the fabric that separates day from night. The order was given to one of the evil fays to go and announce it to her, and to deliver to her the materials required to contrive that masterpiece.

The fay in question was delighted to be charged with that commission; she went to where Florine was and did not neglect the slightest circumstance in carrying it out well. When she arrived, he poor princess was only sustained by the hope that the fay who loved her would not abandon her. Florine listened respectfully to what the fay said to her, and received what she gave her, which consisted of an ebony distaff, an ivory spindle, and spider-webs that were to serve as the fiber to spin the fabric that separates day from night.

"I have no doubt," the fay said to her, "that you were born intelligent and know very well that before placing the fiber on the distaff it is necessary to prepare and beat it, in order to get rid of any dirt it might have picked up. Here is a little stick that you might use; we hope to be able to congratulate you on the beauty of your work and render you justice."

When she had said that, the fay took Florine to the place that had been destined for her labor. It was a cabinet in which the floor, the walls and the ceiling were black marble and the furniture ebony, with a little bed of white damask where the princess would repose. The place only had one little window, very highly-placed, adjacent to the ceiling, which only gave sufficient light to render the place a little less frightful.

The fay left the princess alone in that apartment; she recommended her to be diligent in order to please them, telling that she shared her disgrace and would employ all her credit for her with the queen.

After having examined the place with a glance, Florine laid out her fiber.

As soon as she struck the fiber with her stick, she saw a quantity of large spiders emerge, and, on trying to continue, she realized that someone wanted to doom her. The stick she had been given was sorb wood, which has the virtue of reviving dormant venom.

The princess sighed, and, without succumbing to dolor, sought a means of getting out of the bad situation. She remembered the phial of immortal eau-de-vie that her friend had given her, which expelled poisons; she sprinkled it over her fiber. The spiders immediately disappeared and the fiber became as white as snow.

She took some and put it on her distaff, which she had rubbed with a little of the liquid. Then she started spinning, and covered her spindle with a thread of a delicacy similar to that of the most adroit fays.

The fay who had spoken to the council in Florine's favor, chagrined by what had just been pronounced against her, went to ponder alone in one of the pathways of the garden. Prince Probus, Mauritianne's son, having encountered her there, approached the fay and said: "Sage fay, dare I ask the subject of your sadness? If I can remedy it, I beg you to count on my amity."

The fay felt obliged to reply naturally to such a generous prince; she told him that it was his mother, who had just committed an injustice. Decorum dictated that she make a mystery of it and dissimulate her thinking from it, but as she knew him to have an honest soul, she did not hide it from him that his mother, the queen, had abducted and was keeping prisoner at the court a beautiful princess whose merit was so great that it had attracted the respect and veneration of all humans. She told him that the queen suspected the princess of only having an artificial and studied virtue, in order to steal what only belonged to the fays, and that, holding her council, she had observed there an order so extraordinary and particular that, under an ornament of justice the pretext of discovering the truth, the poor princess had been condemned to spin the fabric that separates day from night.

"There isn't a moment to lose," replied Probus. "That poor princess is going to perish if someone doesn't help her promptly. I'm on my way to salute the queen, who is waiting for me, but I'll come back momentarily. See what we can do to render her in secret all the help she might need."

The fay who had taken Florine to the cabinet of twilight in order to do what she had been ordered, returned there expecting to find her dead, or at least unable to breathe, but she was surprise to find the princess lying on her bed, having finished her work with the utmost perfection.

That first trap, which Florine had avoided so successfully, afflicted the fay, in the fear that she might do as much in the other proofs that might be given to her, and the disturbance and resentment into which that threw her only permitted her to say to Florine: "I'll go and tell the queen that your work is done."

The fay ran to the queen and told her what she had just seen. The queen was momentarily nonplussed. "Someone has given her the necessary advice and help," she said. "There's no need to seek information about that. Send her to me."

That order was carried out immediately. The princess brought her spindle, which she presented to the queen. The queen received it with an expression seemingly replete with kindly sentiments; she praised her and solicited her to continue, assuring her that she would be one of the most eager to want to share her amity.

The queen held a new council and once again found the means to rule that Florine would go in search of the imperial rose without thorns.

One of the fays was delegated to take the princes to the entrance to the road that led to the mountain where the flower in question was found, and she gave her a seed in order to sow another, along with the other things necessary for her journey.

The fay took Florine to the road. "It's here, beautiful princess," she said, "that we must separate; I pray to heaven that the road will guide you fortunately to where you need to go. I've already brought several persons here; some have perished by virtue of their imprudence, and for want of having taken the advice of a fay that you will find on the way; but those who have take it have accomplished what they were ordered to do. Do as she tells you, then, and I shall have the pleasure of seeing you triumphant, with the flower you are going to seek. After having embraced, they separated.

A few paces away the princess found a broad, straight road extending as far as the eye could see through a large wood of palm trees, orange trees and lemon trees. He ground was dotted with all that nature can produce of the sweetest and richest flowers. It was marvelously intercut by an infinity of little streams, which, by their different contours, formed as they fell a soft and charming murmur. By means of their concerts, the birds there inspired everything expressible of the most tender and agreeable.

Florine followed the road without anxiety, and eventually arrived at the end. There she found a huge portico, magnificently constructed, connected to a palace no less superb, where there was a very high tower that was the favorite abode of Rationtine, the fay who was to advise her.

As she approached the portico, the princess perceived the fay in question, who advanced to meet her. She made her many caresses, to which Florine responded as best she could. Rationtine took her into her palace and invited her to sit down on a very rich bed.

The fay only ever went out to meet people who went past her portico, in order to give them sage advice regarding the things they wanted to do. She asked Florine the reason for her journey, to which the princess replied that the council of fays had sent her to seek the imperial rose without thorns.

"You'll succeed in that," said the fay, "if you do as I say. Several have sought it before you; those who have believed me have succeeded; the others have, unfortunately, perished for not having paid attention.

"A little further on, you'll encounter individuals who will seem very agreeable to you, and who will make all kinds of entreaties in persuade you to stay with them. They will try to convince you that they alone enjoy the greatest pleasures of life, but refrain from believing them; they only intend to doom you like themselves; if you pay a little attention to them you'll discover their errors and lies.

"You'll find others who will come to you in order to persuade you of the same things, and are even more dangerous; avoid them promptly and you'll escape from them.

"Finally, you'll encounter other individuals, of a more delicate, insinuating and persuasive intelligence of an extreme finesse, who have the art of winning over and surprising those they see if they listen to them. My princess, as you approach those, imagine that you're entering a very subtle and contagious atmosphere; close all the paths to your heart in order to protect it from their deadly attempts, and convince yourself that in this journey, you only need the imperial rose. Don't take anything the inhabitants offer you; that would be enough to doom you.

"If you're obedient, you'll arrive fortunately at the foot of the mountain where the flower is and you won't fail to find it. I'll give you my son to serve as your guide; although he'll appear to you to be a child, he knows the paths and he'll prevent you from going astray."

"But Madame," said the princess, "Is it an important affair, then, to find this flower? Does it require such a terrible circumspection to succeed in that?"

"It doesn't require as much care as you think," said the fay. "It only requires an honest soul and a firm resolution; I believe you don't lack them, and that's what makes me judge that you'll succeed."

"I suppose," said the princess, "that there are not many people who dare to attempt such an elevated design."

"Don't assume that, my princess," the fay replied. "The adventure is within the range of everyone, and I've seen simple shepherds succeed in it better than kings and queens." As she spoke she took Florine into a room that overlooked a garden of ravishing beauty, where a meal was served that left nothing to be desired of the most exquisite and best prepared.

The princess ate, and at the end of the meal the fay summoned her son to serve as Florine's squire. After great civilities, the princess left in order to continue her journey.

Meanwhile, Mauritianne was desolate that Florine had avoided adroitly, by means of a first proof, the thrust of her hatred, and feared that she might miss her again for the same reasons.

Her friends were no less tormented than her, and while they absented themselves in order to hide their chagrin from the others, the prince and the fay counselor met in one of the arbors in the garden in order to discuss the matter and to try to discover who it might have been that had helped Florine. As their conversation was revolving around that adventure, the fay who was a good friend to Florine arrived and told them that it was her, and the manner in which she had done it even before the condemnation.

The prince and the other fay congratulated her, and felt an incredible joy.

"I can see," said the prince," that this person is of great merit, since she was able, appropriately and without being disconcerted, to make use of the liquid you have given her at such a precious moment, and that she is even better equipped with the beauties of the mind than those of the body."

"There's no doubt about that," said Florine's good friend. "I've seen her in her palace before she came here, and I've always found her brilliant in intelligence and virtue. That, combined with the obligations I have to her, ensures that I will never weary of rendering her all the services I can."

"And I want to second you," said the prince. "She has gone to seek the imperial rose; I want to help her, in order that she can bring the flower back. I'm convinced that it has never been plucked by anyone who merits it more."

After having quit Rationtine, Florine went into a delightful wood, where there were a large number of partly-frayed paths, interlaced with one another; the choice of which to take was unknown to her. Her little guide saw that she was embarrassed, smiled, and took the lead, showing her the one that she ought to take.

The princess was surprised to see a child so assured regarding such a difficult route. "I'm curious to know," she said to him, "how you can be so enlightened."

"I've guided so many different people here," he said, "that those who follow me can't go astray."

"But how can that be the case," said Florine, "being as young as you are?"

"I'm not as young as you think," the guide replied. "I'm as ancient as the first man, and my youth will last as long as there are any in the world. I can't age, being the son of Rationtine, who is a daughter of heaven and who always gives me a flourishing youth."

"But my dear guide," said Florine, "is Madame your mother not of the race of the fays?"

"She is indeed a fay like the others, but of a nobler and more elevated origin than those you have seen. They are only daughters of the stars, and only have power over material and tangible things; my mother, by contrast, is a daughter of heaven ad her power extends over souls; by virtue of her wise counsel, she acts on the will of mortals; that is what has given her the name Rationtine, which means 'princess of reason,' or reason itself. Those who only act on her impulsion can never falter or fail to be happy."

"But since Madame your mother has been sent to us from heaven in order to be so salutary for us," said Florine, "how does it come about that she is always in her palace? There cannot be many people who find it; how many others are there who might profit from her advice if they had the same advantage that I have had?"

"The palace you have seen," said he little guide, "is so well situated that one can arrive there from all the places in the world, and the high tower in which my mother ordinarily resides enables her to be seen distinctly from anywhere. When she sees that someone has need of her she goes to them, or sends me to help them, but her inclination is stronger for those who can find the road that you have taken."

"All those who come to her don't arrive by the same road, then?" said Florine.

"No," said the little guide. "Few people arrive by that road, and many of those who come that way linger there for so long that they only arrive belatedly."

"I'm not surprised by that," said the princess. "It's difficult for a young heart to pass through such an agreeable place at a run."

"You didn't pause there, though," said the little guide, "and everything that is so agreeable in that place didn't deflect you for a moment from the execution of your orders."

"I don't know how that was able to happen," said the princess.

"That's what told my mother that you'd attain the prize of the imperial rose; for, after all, that road so full of charms only represents the pleasures of childhood, where well-born souls don't make a long sojourn, being enthusiastic to arrive before time at my mother's palace; she always shows them an extreme tenderness. It is persons of that sort to whom she gives me as a guide, and recommends to me the most."

As he said that, they emerged from the wood, on the edge of a plain, in which they perceived a few habitations in the distance. In the middle of that plain there was a valley, in the bottom of which there was a river bordered by a wood, the cheerful appearance of which was redoubled in the mirror of the waters, flattering the sight agreeably.

They encountered young people there, lying on the grass in the shade of the boscage. As soon as they saw the princess they got up and came toward her. One of them approached her politely, and said to her: "Would it be permissible for us, Madame, to ask you where you are going? Is it chance that brings you here, and shall we have the pleasure of being useful to you? The sentiments of respect and amity that you inspire in us, Madame, are not ordinary; it is easy to be persuaded, on seeing you, that if you are not a divinity, you must at least be a great princess."

"I'm going to seek the imperial rose without thorns," Florine replied.

"The design is worthy of you, Madame. We're not mistaken in the judgment we've made, and I believe you to be too gracious to refuse to accompany us to a place of refreshment and to stay with us for a few days."

"I can't," said the princess. "My design doesn't permit me to stop. It's the fays who have sent me, and they want to be served promptly."

"It won't cause you any quarrel with them," replied the young woman who had spoken. "They'll understand that you need a few days' rest in order to recover from the fatigues of that great journey. You can't, Madame, encounter on the way an abode more agreeable than ours, nor persons more zealous on your behalf. We're burning with impatience to enable you to share the great pleasures that we enjoy. Do us that honor, Madame, and don't afflict by your refusal persons who are more devoted to you than themselves. We shall soon reach the doors of our palace; we can't suffer that you pass by without refreshing yourself."

All the other ladies who accompanied her joined her, forming a circle, and made pleas so pressing that Florine succumbed to their caresses and their eagerness.

A few steps further on they encountered Ociosine, the princess of the place, who was walking with the members of her court. She greeted Florine graciously, took her to her palace and invited her to sit down beside her in an armchair. Ociosine stretched herself out on a kind of sofa that was placed in a corner of the apartment where they were. The walls and ceiling of the apartment were made of fine glass, and the floor of cedar-wood. The sofa was garnished with large feather cushions covered with silver fabric and surrounded by curtains that formed a sort of niche. Those curtains were made of golden cloth, decorated inside and out with a large number of rubies, diamonds, emeralds and other precious stones.

All the other apartments in the palace were no less magnificent; they were particularly well furnished with a large number of beds, armchairs, cushions, tables, dressing-tables and mirrors. All the members of the court took their places around the princess, in accordance with their various dignities. Ociotine turned to Florine and asked her the reason for her journey. Florine replied that she was seeking the imperial rose without thorns.

"I'm very surprised," said the princess, "that, being so young, you've dared to undertake such a difficult task. It's all that a mature and very strong person can do. Instead of going any further and setting forth inappropriately, stay here for a while and investigate whether the task is above your strength. I have ladies in my court who have taken the same steps that you've just made, and have been obliged by rude fatigues to interrupt the journey in order to take the advice and counsel that is offered to you."

One of the ladies in the circle rose from her seat, addressed Florine and said: "Madame, I am one of the persons to whom the Princess refers. I've passed through Rationtine's palace in order to attempt the same adventure as you, but I didn't get very far before I found an insupportable lassitude and fatigue; I was constrained to sit down, and found myself in a great anxiety as to what I ought to do, when Rationtine's son appeared and came toward me. The child is named Philaphtique; he's very amiable and benevolent. His approach dissipated my troubles; he brought me to the princess you see here, who has a thousand generosities for me, and in whose home there are all sorts of pleasures, while awaiting the time when I have all the strength that I anticipate being necessary to reach the conclusion of such a great design."

As the lady finished speaking, little Philaphtique, whom she had just mentioned, came in, but having perceived Florine's guide with her, he withdrew.

Meanwhile, Princess Ociosine fell asleep in her niche and Florine found herself so exhausted that she did not have the strength to ask her little guide whether the person who had just appeared was his brother.

All the ladies, seeing that their princess was asleep, ran to the things that gave them the most pleasure. Some looked at themselves in the mirrors of their dressing-tables; others lay down on beds or sofas; others took armchairs and gathered together in order to discuss the most beautiful fashions of attire, striking a thousand poses and making contortions of the eyes, hands and feet in order to explain the considerable difficulties of combining properly and diversifying their garments. Others, finally, went to tables were a large number of pieces of cardboard of different colors, assembled very neatly in little piles, which they picked up avidly and to which they imparted a continual agitation, presenting them to one another. They had piles of gold and silver coins in front of them, which followed the movement of the cards, ebbing and flowing.

Florine, who was still beside the queen, and who was unfamiliar with those sorts of amusements, admired the way that the movement of the cards had the power to make such frequent changes, and wanted to know why joy, amour, anger, fury and all the other passions succeeded one another on the faces of the ladies.

Ociosine having woken up, all the ladies returned to her, and a collation of fruits was served, in the most beautiful order in the world. Without emerging from her niche, the princess was able to dispose comfortably of everything on her table. Florine remained in her seat near the princess, attentive to examining everything that happened, sensing terrible agitations in her soul while reflecting on the advice that Rationtine had given her regarding what she saw and what had just been said to her.

While in that mental embarrassment, she was served everything that could be chosen of the best on the table, and, without thinking about what she was doing, she was about to taste it when her little guide deployed two wings that he had on his shoulders, which Florine had not yet perceived. They dispelled from Florine's eyes a black vapor that surrounded her, and as soon as that exhalation had dissipated, Florine recognized that everything she could see was nothing but artifice; that all the fruits were empty or filled with poisonous substances. Immediately, she rose to her feet, and, followed by her guide, she left a place that was so pernicious to her.

On emerging from the confines of the palace, they found an avenue planted with double rows of elms, ash-trees and lindens, which made up a beautiful view. Florine thought at first that it was the road she ought to take, but her little guide stopped her, making her understand that it was necessary not always to go in the direction that seemed most agreeable; that the roads that flatter us most are not usually the most fortunate. He made her quit that road and take one that she saw to the right.

He princess entered a path covered in pebbles, thorns and brambles, where she had great difficulty walking. She could not help saying to her companion: "Why have you obliged me to quit the road that seemed so beautiful, in order to make me take one so rude and difficult?"

"The one you had taken," he guide replied, "leads straight to the Palace of Sensual Pleasure; that is the place my mother told you was so pernicious, where you would have been more at risk than in the Palace of Indolence, which we have just left."

"What obligations I have to you, my dear guide," said Florine. "I'm very sensible to the generosity you have for me; but tell me, please, is there no other milder route on which to continue my journey?"

"This is the shortest way," said the guide. "This road is only difficult at the outset; the others one can take are, in truth, more comfortable, but it's very easy to go astray there, and one finds an infinity of deadly encounters there that one can scarcely avoid."

They arrived a short time later in a plain where the terrain, although ingrate, had become a delightful place by virtue of the care taken to cultivate it. The plain was sown with wheat, and the hills that surrounded it were covered with vines and fruit trees weighed down by their fruit. In admiring such a beautiful place, Florine lost the memory of her fatigues; she testified to her dear guide the joy she felt at having been brought to such a charming place. She took the opportunity to ask whether little Philaphtique, whom she had seen in Ociosine's palace, was his brother, and why he had retired so precipitately.

"He isn't my brother," he replied. "I'm an only son, and my mother has never had any other child than me. She named me Agatonphise, and the individual you saw is only an impostor who, in order to surprise mortals more easily and abuse their simplicity, says that he is my brother, and often even passes himself off as me. It's by that means that he leads those who believe him to their doom. He only came with the design of taking you by surprise, and it was only when he saw that I was accompanying you that he changed his mind."

"I'm not surprised," said Florine, "that he retired so rapidly; one doesn't like to find oneself in the presence of those whom one is pretending to be."

As she finished speaking, they saw a cabin ornamented by bowers covered in Chasselas, Muscat and other exquisite grapes; they saw orchards of vast extent, planted with dwarf trees, in the open, covered with apples and pears, with a large number of trellises edged with peaches and apricots of prodigious size; in another direction there was a huge vegetable garden, where all the leguminous plants useful to life could be seen.

The person who was cultivating the place was named Ergonide. They found him watering it by hand, soliciting nature to give him the abundance that could be seen around him. As soon as he perceived the travelers he came toward them, and after having saluted Florine, he lavished a thousand caresses on Agantophise, who gave him no fewer.

He led them into the shade of an arbor, where he served them a rustic collation of the very best fruits. The princess dared not touch them at first, but when she saw her little guide take some, she ate them, and found the taste marvelous.

When the meal had finished, Ergonide took them to see his menagerie. Florine was charmed by the neatness and beautiful order that she observed there, and seeing that the man did not owe all his wealth to his cares and labors. After many expressions of amity and gratitude, they quit Ergonide and continued their journey.

On the way, Florine conversed with Agatonphise. "That is a man," she said, "who appears to me to be very content and who leads a very tranquil life."

"He labors," said Agatonphise, "and makes such a great pleasure of it that he wouldn't change places with the great kings of the world. He's one of my mother's friends; he often comes to consult us about what he plans to do. He's a son of heaven, like her, and he's the one who informs humans that labor is necessary to prolong their days on earth, and the most assured resource they can have against the indispensable necessities of life."

In the meantime, the princess heard a ritornelle of soft flutes, which flattered the ear sensibly. "How agreeable that music is," she said to Agatonphise. "I feel gripped by joy and a kind of drowsiness that won't permit me to go any further. Wait, I beg you, my dear guide; let's see what it is and where it's coming from."

"Refrain from doing so," he replied. "There's nothing more pernicious for you than stopping here; what gives you so much pleasure would soon horrify you if you knew its cause."

Agatonphise had not finished speaking when a numerous company of people of both sexes appeared, frolicking together in an extravagant manner. The women were semi-naked, shameless and devoid of confusion, and the men, drunk on liquor, had no more modesty or restraint than them.

The princess shivered with dread and horror at the sight of such great disorder, and, seeing them drawing nearer, moved away from them and fled at a surprising speed.

Having drawn away from them and no longer able to see them, Florine stopped momentarily to catch her breath; turning toward Agatonphise, still trembling, she said to him: "These people frightened me badly; I haven't recovered yet."

"You acted prudently," said Agatonphise. "It's only by fleeing that one can avoid the fatal poison of those detestable enchanters, and you wouldn't have had to stay here for long in order to fall into one of their traps, at the risk of dooming yourself like them."

Florine had recovered from her disturbance, and resumed her route, reassured by her faithful Agatonphise. She found herself advancing across a plain that was only limited by a high mountain, which seemed very distant.

The road that led to it was very straight; no stream was visible, nor any shade, nor even any comfortable place to rest.

Florine asked Agatonphise what the mountain was that she could see.

"It's the terminus of your journey," he replied, "the place where the rose can be found for which you've come in search."

The princess quivered with joy at that response, and, believing that she was on the eve of carrying away the imperial rose, she increased her pace and her urgency. The further she went, however, the more it seemed that the mountain drew away from her, which caused her chagrin, impatience and fatigue. The sun, which was shining directly overhead, finished disconcerting her. She resolved to take another road, more agreeable, which presented itself to her left and appeared to lead to the same place as the one she was on.

Not being consulted, Agatonphise let her do it, and Florine continued along that new route, where she found some shade, which she did not think that she could pass up. The unevenness of the ground, however, gradually formed a curtain that hid the mountain from view. She continued nevertheless to march, peevishly and without reflection, and finally reached a village.

The houses, although simply built, were very neat inside. To the entrance to the place the princess found modestly-dressed men who were chatting together in a civil and very reserved manner. They watched her pass by quite indifferently. She encountered others further on, who did not show any more curiosity about her or interest.

Continuing on her way she came into a public square where a woman with a mild and sociable appearance approached her and testified that she was sensible to the anxiety that she seemed to be in, and that she could have confidence in confessing her troubles to her and be persuaded that she would be like a sister to her. It was not simply the sentiments we ought to have for one another that were making her speak, she said, but she felt a natural inclination toward her, of which she could take advantage if she wished. She also insinuated that the place where they were was not suitable for persons of their sex to have a long conversation and begged her to come into her home in order to rest, saying that they could converse at liberty there and say anything comfortably.

Florine believed her and went into her house. At that moment, other ladies came to visit the one whose house she was in, and finding a stranger there as beautiful as the princess, they examined her attentively, looking at themselves in a mirror beside her, and asking her politely where she came from.

"I've come from Rationtine's palace," said Florine.

The ladies sympathized with her and said that she must be fatigued. Then they told her that they would be very glad to hear what she had seen during her journey. Florine told them what had happened to her in Princess Ociosine's palace, what she had seen in Ergonide's farm and the terror caused to her by the frightful company she had encountered.

"Tel me, please," said one of the ladies, "where you desire to go at present?"

"I'm going to look for the imperial rose without thorns," said the princess.

"You can find it in our lands," said the lady, "and since you're occupied with such a noble and great de-

sign, we'll be glad to give you the means to succeed."
They all repeated that, very obligingly.

In the meantime, a man of modest, civil and very polite appearance came in. When he arrived, all the ladies got up hastily in order to offer him their seats. During that ceremony, a maidservant, who seemed no less zealous than the others, brought him a large armchair, which was placed in the best location in the apartment, where he sat down. When he asked discreetly about the subject of their conversation, the lady who had found Florine told him that the stranger he could see had come from Rationtine's palace in order to go in search of the imperial rose; that, as she had entered their village without knowing anyone, she had felt obliged to go and console her and offer her services; and that when he had arrived the lady was telling them about the adventures she had had on the road.

The man turned to Florine and expressed the pleasure that the design in question gave him. After having congratulated her, he told her that she was favored by heaven, having fallen into the arms of that elite society, which had no other passion but hers, and which surpassed infinitely all the other societies of their country in the knowledge of that excellent research; that she could not fail, under their guidance, to carry off that great prize; that, for his part, he shared his care and enlightenment with them as far as was possible, in order to smooth out their difficulties and enable them to overcome generously all the obstacles that might be encountered.

Shortly thereafter, he stood up, made profound civilities to all the ladies, and left.

Those words made no small impression on the mind of the princess; she counted on his promise so much that she flattered herself from then on that she would obtain the flower. That agreeable illusion would have continued if the advice of Rationtine had not alarmed her, by incessantly making her sensible reproaches for her inconstancy and the excessive credulity that she had, to her cost. She was also alarmed to see her dear Agatonphise silent throughout that time, in a sort of torpor from which he did not emerge; that suspended her joy and did not fail to damage slightly the progress that the protector had just made with her.

After the man had gone, one of the ladies said to Florine: "The person who has just left us, Madame, is our guide in the search we are making, like you, for that incomparable flower. He's a man of great probity and profound science, particularly with regard to that discovery. He has the goodness to instruct us and communicate his enlightenment to us, in accordance with the disposition that each of us has to receive it and profit from it. If he has not yet given you precepts on that matter, it's because he anticipates that we won't fail to tell you informally what they are, as he has told us. Be persuaded, Madame, that the flower in question is the symbol of virtue, which renders all those who posses it veritably happy. Some believe that in order to enjoy that treasure, it's necessary to deprive ourselves and extinguish our passions, but they are mistaken and are in error; it is only appropriate to calm them, or to hide them decently, as if they were invisible, and it isn't necessary to deprive oneself of the right that nature gives us and inspires in us."

At that moment, little Philaphtique presented himself to Florine and did what he could to introduce himself next to her. Agatonphise gazed at him with an icy scorn but Philaphtique was not disconcerted.

The lady that had stopped Florine said: "We've been here for a long time; let's go into the other room to refresh ourselves, and we can continue to give this beautiful lady the other enlightenments that will be necessary to her."

They all got up in order to go into that apartment, but Agatonphise, seeing that Florine was about to doom herself like the others, deployed his wings and circled her two or three times; by means of that impetuous movement, he drove away an impure atmosphere that surrounded her and had aided her to deceive herself. Philaphtique was so frightened by it that he fled, and the princess remained alone.

Agatonphise, having seized her by the hand, conducted her to a mountain apart from that place, where he enabled her to remark sensibly the secret communications that land had with the palace of sensual pleasure.

Florine was in an inconceivable sadness at what had just happened to her, and did not know how to express the excessive obligation she had to her dear Agatonphise. She always kept her eyes on him thereafter, her soul having no other desire than to follow him, and she arrived successfully at the foot of the mountain where the flower was.

The foot of the mountain was bordered by cedars and palm trees of great height, and the rock seemed so step that Florine thought that the place was inaccessible and that she would never be able to climb it. She circled around it several times in order to search for a few paths by which to make the ascent, but having found none, she fell into an extreme affliction.

Prince Probus, the son of Mauritianne, did not leave her in that cruel uncertainty for long. He presented himself to her. The prince was known to her because she had seen him in the Palace of the Fays, where he was regard-ed by everyone as a person of great merit; far from the sight causing her any distress, it gave her a secret joy.

"Why, my princess," Probus asked her, "are you not climbing to the summit of this mountain in order to pick the imperial rose, which ought to be the recompense of your labors?"

"I've been searching fruitlessly for a long time, Prince," Florine replied, "for a means of arriving there, and the thing seems impossible to me."

The prince smiled at that response, and said: "Fol-low me, Princess."

Immediately, he went to a tall tree adjacent to the foot of the mountain, and pointed out to Florine that the tree had knots and branches by means of which one could haul oneself up. In fact, he climbed it, and the princess followed him. They went so well from knot to knot and branch to branch that they reached half way, where they found stones disposed in such a manner that they could reach the summit of the mountain comforta-bly.

Florine could not contain her joy at finding herself on the plateau where the flower was that ought to crown her triumph. That extreme pleasure reanimated her spir-its and gave a new splendor to her beauty. She testified to Probus, as a princess, a part of the gratitude she had for the generosity he has just shown her.

"I couldn't fail to render you that small service," Probus said to her. "My inclination for you engaged me to do it, and the fay who is your good friend had in-structed me very well of what I see."

"How grateful I am to that charming fay," cried Florine, "after what she has done for me in having ren-dered such a great prince sensible to my trouble, to the extent of coming in person to free me from a desperate situation in order to lead me to the greatest good fortune."

"Princess," said Probus, "There is the road to go to the Palace of Perseverance, who will show you the flower. I will find you when you return, in order to facilitate the means of returning you promptly to my mother's palace."

The princess followed the road and arrived at the palace, where she found Perseverance, who welcomed her agreeably and led her to the flowery field where the precious pledge was. It would be difficult to explain the sentiments of pleasure and joy that the princess had at the sight of that treasure. The dread that she had in gazing at it that her eyes might be deceiving her again made her grasp that incomparable flower avidly, and the earth, in seeing itself deprived of it, seemed changed; its bosom opened, which served it as a mouth in order to say to Florine that she ought at least to console it. Seeing in a moment that place so well prepared to receive insemination, the princess remembered the seed that she had brought. She sowed in the same place from which she had just plucked the flower, and had the pleasure of seeing nature reproduce one exactly similar to the one she had.[4]

---

[4] The symbolism of this passage seems odd, to say the least; combined with the tall tree and the role of the prince in enabling her to climb it, a Freudian would have no difficulty decoding it in sexual terms, but that might be difficult to reconcile with the episode in the village, which seems to reject the "calm passion" offered by conventional marriage quite explicitly. On the other hand, a constant theme of *contes de fées* is the conflict generated by attempts being made to force hero-

Having the imperial rose, Florine no longer thought of anything but returning, and took the road by which she had come. Prince Probus, who was waiting for her, seeing her take that route, stopped her and said: "That route would take too long, Princess. Then too, one never returns with that flower via the same place from which one has had the advantage of picking it. Let's take a shorter route." Having given her his hand, he took her via a very agreeable place, and she found herself, insensibly, not far from the Palace of the Fays.

Renown immediately published the news to the court of the fays that Florine had returned, charged with the precious treasure. The good fays could not contain their joy, and Mauritianne saw herself obliged to admit publicly that Florine merited a recompense worthy of her labors.

Florine was still advancing her return under the conduct of the prince, but when they were close enough to the palace, Probus said to her: "It's necessary that I quit you, my princess, for fear of being seen. You're on the right path, and you can no longer go astray.

The princess continued on her way, raising her eyes to the heavens to render thanks for the favors that he had received.

Mauritianne had already assembled her council; where it had been decided that Florine would be received with great magnificence.

As soon as Florine appeared at the gates of the palace, Mauritianne, accompanied by her entire court, came to meet her, presenting her with a chariot, into which she

ines into arranged marriages in spite of their commitment to finer lovers.

obliged her to climb. The chariot was gold, richly wrought and drawn by four beautiful white horses, variously caparisoned. The first caparison was covered with sapphires, the second with various precious stones, including agates, onyxes, topazes and rubies, the third with diamonds and the fourth with amethysts of an inestimable value. Four fays were guiding the horses with reins woven of gold and silk.

The princess entered the palace with that equipage to the joyful cries of all the fays. At the foot of the great staircase, Mauritianne offered her a hand to help her descend from the chariot, and conducted her into a hall where a considerable repast was served, which passed with much evidence of joy at her fortunate return. Afterwards, she was taken to one of the finest apartments in the palace in order to repose.

The next day, Florine was taken with the same pomp and magnificence to the temple dedicated to Virtue, which was not far from the palace, in order to thank heaven for the favor that it had shown her during the journey. There she deposited the flower she had brought and received a crown from the hand of Mauritianne, which she took from that altar consecrated to Virtue.

When Florine had returned to the palace and retired to the apartment prepared or her, the counselor fay, her good friend and Prince Probus came to see her in order to congratulate her in private and express the joy they felt at her elevation.

"It's not to me," the princess said, "that the praise you're attributing to me is due; it's to the powerful aid that you've given me, and particularly to this generous prince; all my labors would have been futile, and without him I'd still be at the foot of the mountain, deprived forever of being able to pick the flower that had given me the sweet felicity of seeing you again."

"Could I refuse that feeble aid," said the prince, "to a princess whom heaven has always protected? In addition, does not natural law inspire us and order us to relieve those we see in need of it?"

"There are few people," said the princess, "who have such precious sentiments, and even if it is so, do I owe any less to the excess of generosity that you had in saving me yourself, when another could have done it if you had ordered him to do so."

The discussion continued for some time of the gratitude that Florine expressed for the cares that had been given to her; she begged them to continue.

"Our duty obliges us to that," said the counselor fay. "We are only sent to earth to defend those who are persecuted unjustly."

After a long conversation they left Florine alone in order to rest from her long fatigue. As her good friend left, she said: "Have no fear, my dear princess; live in repose; no one can harm you any longer."

"But I'm not yet in my palace," said Florine."

"Time will bring all things," the fay replied, "and we shall look after your interests so well that you'll have reason to be satisfied."

Florine thanked her for all her cares, and begged her always to be favorable, which the fay promised again. After embracing her, she went to join the other two, who had left and were waiting for her, walking slowly.

Prince Probus and the counselor fay, seeing her arrive, proposed that they go for a walk together in one of the palace gardens, in order to talk about everything that had happened on the subject of Florine. They could not weary of admiring her merit, especially the prince, who praised it so highly that it gave the good fay, Florine's friend, reason to believe that the prince was in love with her. She felt a secret joy at that, hoping that it would be useful to the princess.

In order to be more assured, seeing that the prince was continuing to praise her, she said: "Prince, I believe that in the eulogy you've just given the princess there is something more than admiration; if I'm not mistaken, there's also a little inclination and amity."

The prince blushed, which gave the two fays reason to laugh, and the sage counselor fay spoke, saying that it was not surprising; that it would be difficult to see such great merit without holding it in esteem, and that from esteem to amour the slope was very slippery and hard to resist; that if that were the case, it could not be criticized; on the contrary, it would be just as surprising if his soul were limited to esteem alone.

"You would approve, then, sage fay," said the prince, "of any love I might have for the princess?"

"Yes," she replied, "and you ought not to doubt it."

The prince could not help confessing then that he had all the amour for the princess by which a sensible heart could be set ablaze.

"It is by those features," said the fay, "that I recognize the great Probus. You have performed splendid actions before, but this one crowns all the others. To love a persecuted virtue is an action without equal, and worthy of you."

"But what will that amour serve me?" said the prince. "The person who is the cause of it is unaware of it, and I cannot consent to her being informed, for fear of displeasing her."

"Have no fear," said Florine's friend. "The road from gratitude to tenderness is as slippery and as short as the one from esteem to amour."

"How agreeably you flatter my passion, beautiful fay," replied the prince, "But tell me, I beg you, if that were so, would I not still have everything to fear and a great obstacle to overcome? Would my mother approve of my passion, if she saw that it was for a person against whom her hatred is never-ending?"

"Heaven disposes of things as it pleases," said the counselor fay. "It is necessary to hope that, approving of your sentiments for the princess, it will give you the means to execute them. I foresee that we will soon see some considerable events at the court. Florine's glory has given the queen a cruel reverse. She might be striving to hide it, but she still feels the chagrin of failing to doom her very keenly. I have found her in one of the arbors of the garden, alone with one of her confidantes. They seemed to me to be pensive and very embarrassed, which made me judge that they are meditating some great design. In the meantime, prince, hide your sentiments, and make sure that Florine knows nothing about them. Only continue to render her all the services you can; that is as much as you can do to arrive at the happiness you desire."

PART TWO

The counselor fay was not mistaken in judging that Florine's glory had given rise to terrible emotions in Mauritianne's soul. She retreated every day with her confidante to the most isolated places in the gardens of her palace in order to talk to her about her dolor.

"You can see," she said to her, "whether I have reason to be afflicted. All the measures I took to doom that mortal who is odious to me have only served only served to augment her good fortune, my confusion and my despair. I wanted to persecute her and cause her to perish without revealing my fury, and I found myself forced to prepare her triumph and crown her with my own hand. Disastrous ambition, why have you brought me to where I am, to make me suffer such cruel pains? Let us return to the places where I was omnipotent; let us get away from a council that is opposed to everything that flatters my passions without my having the liberty to lament it. Even my son disapproves of my conduct, because he has been brought up in this court. You see me condemned by almost everyone, and people only defer in appearance to the respect that is due to the splendor that surrounds me. Let us return to Feliciane a throne from which I cast her down; it will even be glorious for me to set her back on it. Let us go live in the places where I established an empire that made everyone tremble under my laws. Imprudent as I was, my passion blinded me to the point of not knowing, when I saw that princess, that her virtue was solid and that heaven favored her."

"But if the princess overcame the obstacles that she encountered," said the confidante, "it was only by virtue of Rationtine's advice."

"That's true," retorted the queen, "but Rationtine is only where she is in order to give advice, and it is an order of heaven that she's executing when she warns those who go to find her. An infinite number of persons pass by, and although she instructs them, the number of those who follow her advice is so small that the princess is almost the only one who has been able to profit from it. Neither the charms of Ociosine's palace nor any of the other obstacles she encountered stopped her; she reached the foot of the mountain where the flower was, and heaven, by means of unexpected and marvelous aid, gave her the means to climb it."

"Might it not have been one of the fays who helped her to reach the top of the mountain," said the confidante, "and if that were the case, would you not have the right to punish her and annihilate what you have done for Florine as a conquest contrary to the rules?"

"No," said Mauritianne. "Don't you know that we are only on earth to protect virtue? That princess has too much of it; that's what unchained my wrath against her, because she doesn't belong to the fays, which informs mortals that they can be virtuous without us. If I could discover which of the fays has given her aid, would I not be obliged to praise her and to recompense her for it?"

"I can see," said the confidante, "that it is very difficult to oppress the virtuous without appearing unjust."

"That is what makes my torment," interjected the queen. "I was too precipitate. Florine is now shielded from the proofs to which I could still have subjected her, and to which she might have succumbed. I no longer have any but one means to flatter my hopes, and that is to solicit her, to persuade her—for its necessary that she wants to do it—to go to seek Queen Feliciane in the Marvelous Labyrinth. As she has not been warned about the perils she would find there, she might perhaps generously engage to do it. "

"But if Florine came back with Queen Feliciane," said the confidante, "you'd be obliged to surrender the crown you hold to her."

"I don't care," said Mauritianne. "After what's happened, it's indifferent to me whether I stay here or return to my islands. But it would be agreeable to me to doom her! Then I'd be delivered of a person I can't abide. You know that when someone has entered that labyrinth, they can't get out again without Princess Feliciane. Take the trouble, then, to assemble the council, and I'll summon Florine, in order to engage her to execute this design."

When the council was assembled, Mauritianne said to the members: "My sisters, we have recently given Princess Florine the prize that is due to her virtue; I believe that, being above all the obstacles that ill fortune might oppose to her designs, she might also be able to liberate Feliciane. I would have an extreme joy in seeing her mount the throne again. I have desired that for a long time, in order also to return to what is mine, which I cannot do if she is not here. If Princess Florine wishes, she can do anything. Is it not your opinion, my sisters, that she should be asked to come here and that the proposition should be put to her? Join with me, I beg you, and let us engage her, if we can, in this noble design. It would bring about the liberty of a great queen, unfortunately exiled, who can only be delivered by a fortunate mortal."

When the queen had finished speaking, the assembly did not respond immediately; all the fays were occupied in wondering what the queen might have in mind that had caused such a great change in her. The fays could see clearly that her jealousy of Florine was not extinct, but they could not understand why Mauritianne wanted to engage Florine once again in an affair that might conclude as fortunately as the others, and thus exposing her to losing a crown that had cost her so much.

One of the fays of Mauritianne's party broke the silence, and said that if Florine wanted to excuse herself it would be appropriate to constrain her, that violence was just where mildness could not do anything, particularly on this occasion.

"What you are advancing," said Mauritianne, "is unjust. Princess Florine is, like us, at liberty to accept what I propose or to refuse it. If it had been permitted for fays to undertake this project, the queen would have returned a long time ago; I would have gone to search for her myself; but since it is necessary for a mortal to accomplish it, where could we find one better than Florine?"

The sage fay counselor said that it was true that Florine had the dispositions necessary for the success of that great design, but that, even with all those rare qualities, there were certain perils that would require extraordinary aid in order to provide protection from them.

The queen said that she did not oppose the princess being given that aid, and that the fays could follow their inclination for her in that. With that, it was agreed that she be asked to come to the council. Two of the principal fays were sent to make her compliments on behalf of the others.

Florine came. Mauritianne had sent two more fays to meet her, and they all conducted her to the queen, who had her given a seat beside her on the same platform on which the throne was placed.

When Florine had sat down, Mauritianne spoke to her thus: "The conduct you have shown, incomparable princess, in the conquest of the imperial rose, persuades us that you are capable of executing the greatest designs, and that there are no obstacles that can limit the endeavors you undertake. There is still one considerable means of signaling your heroic virtue. Our great Queen Feliciane has been exiled for a long time in the Marvelous Labyrinth; she can only be released from it by a mortal like you. Beautiful princess, render liberty to that dear queen. Enter the labyrinth and bring her out. All the fays, like me, beg you and implore you to do it with the strongest entreaties. This is a means, my princess, of acquiring even more glory than in the conquest you have just made; it is a double crown that heaven is presenting to you and I believe that your generous heart will not be able to refuse."

Florine listened to the queen attentively, and replied: "Madame, the honor that you propose to me of going in search of Queen Feliciane and obliging all the fays would make me attempt anything; but Madame, it is not to a simple mortal like me that that deliverance is reserved. Although I plucked the imperial rose, that action is possible to all those who wish to undertake it and follow the advice of Rationtine. It is not the same with Queen Feliciane; that is a grace that can only be accorded to a person chosen by heaven itself, which it wanted to favor. So I beg you, Madame, to dispense me of this honor."

The queen tried to persuade her then that the celestial powers had destined her to deliver the queen and that she could not oppose their will without attracting the wrath of heaven.

While Mauritianne made that reply adroitly, Florine looked attentively at all the fays, one after another, in order to penetrate their sentiments and to judge what she ought to resolve. She thought she could see, in the eyes of the sage counselor, that she would be very glad if she were to accept the task, but, for fear of being mistaken, she asked for time in order to respond, which was granted to her.

When the session was ended, Florine was escorted back to her apartment by all the fays, who implored her to return their queen to them.

When Florine had been taken back to her apartment, Mauritianne shut herself in her own in order to dream agreeably about the new trap that she had set for Florine; she still flattered herself secretly that she might succumb to the large number of reefs that she would encounter in the labyrinth in question, and her only dread was the uncertainty she still had as to whether Florine would accept the commission.

Prince Probus, having heard about the proposal that his mother had just made Florine, went in search of the fay counselor in order to discuss with her the means that might best enable Florine to carry out the project successfully. He found her alone on the bank of the canal in the palace garden, thinking, like him, about the powerful aid that she might be given.

As soon as the fay perceived the prince she went to met him. "What reasons you have to rejoice, Prince!" she said to him. "It has been proposed to Florine to go and bring Feliciane out of the labyrinth she is in. What happiness there would be for you in that circumstance, if it is true that you have as much amour for the princess as you have declared!"

"If you doubt it, sage fay," the prince replied, "you are doing me an injustice, for…."

"I would be convinced of it," the fay interrupted, "if you serve Florine to the prejudice of your mother."

"I could perhaps abandon the princess if there were any justice in my mother's resentments," said the prince, "but as Florine is being persecuted unjustly, even if I had no passion or her, I would do everything that I plan to do."

"Whatever I might have said, my prince," the fay replied, "I have always believed what you are telling me, and that is what has made me resolve to engage Florine to accept this proposition. I'm convinced that, with your help, she will have the advantage of delivering Feliciane, and that you will also find by virtue of that new means for forming bonds of eternal gratitude.

"As Florine had not yet accepted the proposal that had just been made to her, they went to her apartment together, in order to discover what her latest sentiments were.

Having entered the apartment, they found her with her good friend, who was soliciting her to return Feliciane to them. Seeing them arrive, that fay said to them: "Come and persuade the princess; she doubts the ability she has, and is hesitating to accept the glory of going to liberate the exiled queen."

"Madame," said the prince, "I cannot believe that you would refuse to be the worthy liberator of that queen, so much desired."

"What, Prince!" retorted Florine. "You, who know my weakness, and the difficulty I have just had in plucking the imperial rose, would also engage me in this new design, which is even more difficult and in which I would doubtless perish?"

"Is it possible, my princess," said the fay counselor, "that you would have the harshness to refuse Probus, this zealous prince, who desires as we do the liberation of the queen? Perhaps your soul has the weakness of believing that this great prince might abandon you to the various obstacles that might oppose it? If you think so, my princess, be disabused; his sensitive and generous soul would not permit him to do that and he has the greatest interest in your success. For our part, my princess, we will be with you, with the urgent desire to see you return with Queen Feliciane."

Florine saw herself forced, in the end, by gentle violence, to respond to the sentiments of the prince and the two fays. She promised them that she would go to search for Queen Feliciane, and that she would do it on the basis of the confidence she had in them. They went away full of joy.

The delay given to the princess to respond having elapsed, the council of fays reassembled and Florine was summoned to it. She was conducted to where she had been before; when she was seated, the queen said to her: "Well, Madame, might we hope that you will go to remove Queen Feliciane from her exile?"

"Madame," replied Florine, "although the design might be far above anything I can do, and the little experience I have tells me that there is nothing for me to hope for in this occasion but fatal consequences, the strong inclination that I have to oblige you has prevailed. If my efforts are futile, it will still be glorious for me to be deprived of life for such a noble aim. I shall depart, Madame, when you do me the honor of ordering me to do so."

That response spread universal joy through the assembly, and all the fays made thousands of wishes advantageous for Florine. There was nothing anywhere but pleasures and diversions because Florine had accepted the proposition.

When everything that Florine could carry with her was ready, the prince went to see her and said to her: "My princess, as you are on the point of departure, here is a ring that I am giving you; keep it on your person. By means of that ring I shall see all the perils you are facing, in which you might have need of aid. As soon as you have put it in your mouth, I will be beside you."

The princess received that present, which served to augment her confidence more than a little.

The provisions that were given to Florine to make the journey were prepared; they were easy to carry, for the aliments were so nourishing that very little needed to be taken in order to sate and fortify her.

All the fays went to fetch Florine from her apartment and accompany her until she was some distance from the palace, making the echoes repeat their cries of joy. The queen embraced Florine, wishing her a prompt return and the greatest prosperity. Then the two fays who were to conduct her to the entrance of the road leading to the labyrinth departed with her in order to go there, and the fay counselor and her good friend also went a further few paces with Florine in order to embrace her.

When the two fay guides had arrived with Florine and the entrance to a great wood they said: "Beautiful princess, it's here that we must separate; we pray to heaven that it will give you the strength to enter the labyrinth where you are going and to bring back our great queen. Follow this path; it will take you to the labyrinth." Then they saluted her and took the road back to the palace.

Florine went into the wood and followed the route that had been indicated to hr. How many reflections she made in that solitude with a view to the combats she was about to sustain! Far from being afflicted, however, she was only occupied by the thought of vanquishing them, with the help of the prince and the two fays.

After having passed through the wood, she found herself in a plain punctuated by a few rocks. On the rocks Florine saw a few sparse flocks, which were grazing tranquilly, but there was no one taking the trouble to guard them. As she continued walking she perceived in a concavity in one rock a small cabin covered in straw, interlaced with a few tree branches, which engendered a desire to go there. Scarcely had she taken a few steps in that direction when a young shepherdess came out clad in a pale gray fabric, with a crook in her hand and a straw hat on her head to protect her from the ardor of the sun.

They approached one another, and Florine was surprised to find, in such great simplicity, the most gracious and noblest bearing and manners in the world.

"May heaven give you what you want, beautiful shepherdess," Florine said to her, "and heap you with its favors."

"And may it guide you fortunately to the goals of your desires, beautiful princess," said the shepherdess.

"I'm obliged to you, my shepherdess," said Florine, "for the great advantages you wish for me. Alas, without the grace of heaven, I cannot finish what I intend to do."

"If your design is just," said the shepherdess, "and you have confidence in it, it will not deceive you; whatever obstacles oppose you, they will all fail and you will arrive at the goal you have set yourself. But my princess, you seem fatigued; come into my cabin to rest; there, perhaps, I can tell you something that might be useful to you."

Florine accepted her offer, and when she had gone in the shepherdess invited her to sit down. After a few civilities, she said to her: "The interest that I am taking in everything regarding you, my beautiful princess, also makes me take the liberty of asking you the reasons that have brought you to this solitude, which is almost unknown to mortals."

"Most amiable shepherdess," replied Florine, "I have been engaged by Queen Mauritianne to go in search of Queen Feliciane in order to bring her back from the exile she is in."

"I wasn't mistaken on seeing you," said the shepherdess. "I thought that might be your design. Oh, princess, how heaven is preparing you for glory and happiness if you bring back that great queen. According to the edict of the supreme intelligences, that deliverance is only reserved for a fortunate mortal, and it appears that it is you. Don't be deterred, my princess, in all the difficult paths you find, and you'll doubtless overcome them. Pardon me, my princess, for the transports of joy in which you see me; they depart from an excess of tenderness that I have for the dear queen of whom you are going in search."

"Are the obstacles that are in this labyrinth so very difficult to overcome, then?" Florine asked her.

"No, my princess," said the shepherdess. "They become facile when strong resolution makes them scorned."

Florine asked her then why Queen Feliciane had been exiled.

"That," the shepherdess replied, "is a long story. In order to instruct you, I must tell you, my princess, that when Queen Feliciane reigned, everything was perfectly tranquil in our lands. My sisters and I were her dearest favorites, and it was by way of our sisters that she gave mortals that mild felicity. One of my sisters was named Achakie, the other Pisonide, and I am Simpliciane, Achakie was the one who preserved them against avid and tumultuous desires, which rob quietude and pleasure of a veritable security. Pisonide inspired them with amity, good faith and an inviolable fidelity to one another, and I lifted them up again when they fell into the weakness of believing that one needs a great many different things in order to be happy.

"That order was so well-established that we only had to appear before the people to whom the queen sent us in order to recall some and reanimate others successfully. Those people testified so much respect and veneration to us that they did not believe that they could live without us. Those times, my princess, would still endure but for the extraordinary adventure about which you are about to hear.

"There was in our vicinity a rather handsome young man named Hypopsite; he was the son of Zelopie, but he was not as nasty-minded as her. His respectful and easy manners gave him a facile entry into many houses. Coming to ours as he went to the others, Pisonide pleased him, and gradually, he became so amorous that he no longer had the strength to dissimulate his passion. He explained himself to her in terms so vivid and respectful that, although my sister had no disposition to listen to him, she had a secret compassion for him. However, she responded sharply everything that might be capable of disabusing the most amorous and stubborn man in the world.

"He was not put off, and continued his assiduities with regard to my sister, giving her new evidence of his attachment every day, which engaged Pisonide to pay some attention to it. After having examined the matter, though, she saw clearly that if she married Hypopsite, not only would he be able to subject her to rude ordeals himself, but he would also expose her to all the violent excesses of his mother Zelopie, which caused her to resolve to send Hypopsite away.

"One day, when he wanted to make my sister hear his complaints again, she replied to him that she did not want to marry, that it was a firm decision, that she had already told him that everything he might do would be futile, and that she begged him to withdraw. Hypopsite, who was very much in love, replied to her that if she was speaking seriously he would kill himself in despair. As that is a fashion in which lovers often talk, Pisonide paid no attention to it and repeated to him that he must be convinced by what she said, that they were her true sentiments.

"Hypopsite went away, and came back, as usual. My sister, fatigued, begged the queen to send her to a distant place inaccessible to Hypopsite. Feliciane sent my sister to where she wanted to go, but the young man, finding himself deprived of seeing her, also went to see the queen and begged her to be favorable to him. He made her a confession of the purity of his sentiments and everything he had done to engage my sister to respond to his desires, and he begged the queen to oblige Pisonide to accept his heart.

"Feliciane replied to him that all our actions ought to be just and devoid of constraint, that Pisonide might have a natural aversion for him even though he felt amour for her; that it was easy for him to know that by virtue of her refusals and that it would be a great injustice to want to engage her to accept a heart that did not suit her.

"As the young man was violent, that response out him in despair, and without heeding anything but his fury, he left the queen and climbed a rock, from which he threw himself into the stormy sea of desires, where his life and his passion were extinguished.

"The rumor of that death having spread, his mother, who was no less violent than him, became furious, and only respired the subtle poison of a cruel vengeance. Zelopie went to find Mauritianne and paid court to her, in order to engage her to take up her interests, and to agree with her means of dooming her enemies and her son's.

"Mauritianne received that afflicted mother and judged it appropriate to do what could be done to oblige people to carry their complaints to the superior intelligences and to make them say that Feliciane and Pisonide had caused the death of their intimate friend Hypopsite, from whom they had received great services. That succeeded perfectly. The avaricious, the ambitious and the vindictive signed the petition.

"The supreme intelligences received that petition and, in order to be certain of the truth, they summoned Mauritianne's companions to inform them. That was done secretly, and the whole procedure was complete before Feliciane and we knew anything about it.

"The information was taken to the intelligences, and whatever care was taken to make the queen and my sister seem criminal, the intelligences, who cannot be deceived, knew the innocence of the accused and the character of the others. The intelligences, irritated by the procedure of the accusers and wanting to punish them, were discussing together the means of doing so with an equitable verity when one of them suggested that, in order to judge the ingrates who, after having received so many benefits from the queen and my sister, had had the temerity to accuse the unjustly, the best thing to do was to grant them what they demanded: to send the queen and my sister into the Marvelous Labyrinth and to give them Mauritianne to govern them. She added that felicity was an inseparable companion of Feliciane, and where Feliciane was not, trouble, inconstancy and disorder would always reign, and by that means, they would be the artisans of their own misfortune.

"That advice was taken by all the intelligences; Queen Feliciane and my sister were sent into the Marvelous Labyrinth, to remain there until a mortal was found who had the strength to enter it and overcome all the obstacles that opposed the emergence of the queen, and in the meantime, Mauritianne would govern in her stead.

"The queen and my sister obeyed that edict and went into the labyrinth, where they still are. The queen also took Achakie with her, and left me to take care of what might still concern her here. I chose this retreat, and my greatest pleasure is conducting the flocks that you see."

When the shepherdess had finished speaking, Florine said to her "What you have just told me augments the desire I have to liberate Feliciane so strongly that I shall only breathe henceforth for that extreme satisfaction; that pleasure will be so great for me that it will enable me to scorn all the obstacles that threaten to make me perish."

The shepherdess had an inconceivable joy in seeing Florine in those sentiments. She served the princess a collation of the best things she had, and then Florine resumed her route. Simpliciane accompanied her for some time, and when she quit her she drew her attention to a large clump of trees in the distance, which served to decorate the entrance to the labyrinth.

The princess continued walking and arrived at the labyrinth, which had two large interlaced cedars at its entrance, the branches of which formed a kind of huge portico. She went through it, and continued her route along a narrow path, which took her to a large open space where a considerable number of paths ended.

The princess remained in that place for some time without being able to decide which of the paths she should take. As she was in that anxiety, fortunately for her, two women appeared, one of whom was clad in white so bright that it dazzled the gaze; the other's attire was no less beautiful, but she had in addition a very bright sky-blue mantle. Those ladies had an air of majesty that made it evident that their rank was very distinguished.

"What are you looking for?" the ladies asked Florine as they drew nearer to her.

"The unique desire to liberate Queen Feliciane has bought me here," Florine told them, "but I'm very embarrassed, and I'd like to know that I haven't gone astray, and which of these paths I ought to follow."

"If you want to find that good queen," replied the ladies, "take the road to your right. It might perhaps appear difficult to you, but it's the most reliable. Always remember, beautiful princess, that it's necessary not to turn back; in this place the terrain changes incessantly, and the paths you think are the ones you have just followed are others that will lead you to frightful precipices."

Florine begged them to tell her to whom she owed that good advice.

"My name is Pisonide," said the one who had spoken, "and this is Achakie."

"What a pleasure it is for me to encounter you," said Florine, "after having seen the shepherdess Simpliciane. What ought I not to hope for my journey, having had the good fortune to encounter the two favorites of the benevolent queen for whom I have come to search? But can it be chance that I ought to thank for such a fortunate encounter?"

"It's our sister Simpliciane," Pisonide and Achakie replied, "who told us that you were in the labyrinth, and who engaged us to come to extract you from the embarrassment you might be in as to which path you ought to take; but now that you know that, my princess, we'll go tell the queen that you're searching for her. Have no doubt, beautiful princess, that she will favor you. Only continue, and we shall have the joy of seeing you return to the palace when you have accomplished what you must do."

Pisonide and Achakie having retired, Florine took the path that had just been indicated to her. She found it covered in slippery pebbles, which caused her to fall continually. The path was only surrounded by sterile ground, which produced nothing but thistles and brambles. The route could only be followed by climbing or descending incessantly.

Eventually, Florine, overwhelmed by fatigue and having a pressing need to take some nourishment, was obliged to sit down on a rock she found. She was surprised, however, when she saw that she had lost the provisions she had been given, and was sad to find herself in a remote desert with nothing to eat and without the hope of finding anything.

As she was making those afflicting reflections a woman came toward her, who was badly dressed with a melancholy and chagrined physiognomy, followed by another woman whose lively and easy manner compensated somewhat for the faults of her attire.

"Who are you?" Florine said to them. "If you are inhabitants of this place, give me, I beg you, something to eat,"

"My name is Anackire," said the first. "I don't have the ability to help you, but here is my daughter Philopone, who can."

Philopone had no sooner heard her mother speak than she set forth to search for some assistance for the princess. She brought her some wild fruits, which Florine ate with as much appetite as the ones offered to her in the abode of Ergonide.

When the princess was slightly refreshed, she continued on her way. Philopone offered to accompany her, which was a great help to her; from time to time, she bought Florine some subsistence.

As they advanced through that desert, Florine asked Philopone whether it was still a long way to where Feliciane was. The latter replied that sometimes the road was short and at others very long, resulting from the various changes that happened to the terrain.

From time to time Florine made sensible reflections on the state in which she found herself. The loss of her aliments was one of the most serious, and all the aid that Philopone gave her could not console her for it.

In the meantime, a man called Grilison appeared, who followed her, trying to persuade her by means of a thousand irritating arguments that she merited all the trouble she was having.

"Were you not quite happy in the Palace of the Fays," he said, "after having avoided such a great number of perils in the conquest you had just made? Was it necessary to engage yourself recklessly in this new design? Where are those friends now on who you were counting, and the great help they ought to be giving you? The prince and the others are amusing themselves at court without thinking about you, and without Philopone you'd already be dead."

Florine suffered considerably from having that man incessantly plaguing her ears. She tried to get rid of him, but he always began again. Seeing that the man was insupportable to Florine, Philopone sought all means to console her. The poor princess could do no more; that discourse was giving her more difficulty than anything she had felt during her journey.

Fortunately, another man arrived carrying a spade. Having recognized him as Ergonide, Florine ran to meet him. "You've arrived just in time," she told him, "I'm in urgent need of your help. Give me news of my dear Agatonphise and tell me, I beg you, why he has abandoned me."

"He hasn't abandoned you," said Ergonide. "He's the one who sent me here to give you pleasure. But my princess, what are you doing with that man I see following you, who is more capable of driving you to despair with his discourse than consoling you?"

"What you say is true," said the princess. "He's following me against my will; he's so insupportable and fatigues me so much that I no longer know where I am. I've tried to get rid of him, but he still follows me."

"I'll rid you of him," said Ergonide, taking his spade and striking the man on the back with it, who fled at such great speed that he did not give himself time to complain. Then Ergonide turned over a large square of land with his spade, in which he sowed seeds that he had brought. He presented delicious fruits to the princess, summoned Hypomone to keep her company, and then withdrew.

Although Ergonide had come to Florine's aid, Philopone had not quit her. She loved the princess so much that she sought incessantly for new means of being useful to her. Every day she aided Florine to cultivate the ground that Ergonide had prepared for her, which produced everything she needed to shield her from the insults of time. Hypomone disposed the mind of the princess so well that she lived with the same pleasure that she had had at the fays' court. She did not believe that she had ever been as tranquil and as happy as she was in that solitude.

Only one thing embarrassed her, and that was the sojourn she was making there, which was delaying her arrival at Feliciane's palace in order to liberate the queen. She confided that to Hypomone, who told her that she ought not to worry about it, that the advancement of her journey did not always consist of walking, but of making good use of all the difficulties she encountered; that heaven would give rise to frequent changes that would enable her to get closer to Feliciane's palace, which was the veritable means of finding the queen.

Florine was so consoled by what Hypomone told her that she no longer thought about anything but cultivating her garden, and her solitude became a delightful abode for her. When she was weary of the cultivation of her garden she walked in the surrounding area, sometimes alone but more often with her two companions.

One day they showed her a rock from which one could see a large terrain. Florine was charmed by the place, especially the beauty of a palace that was offered to her sight. Florine asked Hypomone what the palace was that seemed so beautiful; Hypomone replied that it was Feliciane's palace, and the place where it was necessary to go.

"Well, my princess," Hypomone continued, "You can see that you're getting close to it and that you aren't as far away from it as you thought. But it's here that it's necessary to arm yourself with a new constancy and strong resolutions. Don't flatter yourself, my princess, there are still many labors and difficulties to endure before reaching that palace, but when you've overcome them, you'll enter into that happy abode and you'll enjoy the extreme satisfaction of seeing Feliciane in all the splendor of her grandeur."

Florine listened with great pleasure to everything that Hypomone said to her; she found a salutary unction that rendered her almost insensible to the afflictions of her hindrances.

From that time on, all the princess's excursions took her to the rock, and every time she went there it seemed to her that she was getting closer to Feliciane's palace, or that it was getting closer to her.

One day, when she was contemplating the objective of her desires, she saw an agreeable young man coming toward her, clad in crimson velvet. Florine was surprised to see the young man in such a solitary place. As he approached her he said: "Madame, you're admiring the beauty of Feliciane's palace."

"That's true," said Florine, "and the desire to go there is what occupies me entirely."

"That's a glorious design, Madame," said the young man, "and it's the means of arriving at a veritable happiness. A long time ago I proposed to go there myself but I can't do it alone. It's necessary for me to find a few people who have the same passion as me I've already encountered several who were burning with impatience at first to go there, and who promised me the most beautiful things in the world, but at the first difficulties they found they were put off and abandoned me. That, Madame, is why I haven't reached Feliciane's palace and why I'm wandering in this place, still searching for someone who has the same design as me. If you want to go and find Queen Feliciane and would like me to accompany you, I promise you that, whatever might happen, I won't quit you."

Feliciane thought that the young man, who had said that his name was Psiphismate, might be of some use to her. She had heard mention of him in very advantageous terms. She told him that she accepted the offer he had made to share the cares of the journey with her, on condition of not abandoning her.

"It isn't me," said Psiphismate, "who lacked fidelity to those I've accompanied; it's them who abandoned me."

As he said that he sat down next to Florine on the rock where she was and conversed with her about the means of reaching the fortunate palace.

Some time afterwards a man with a bizarre, anxious and violent physiognomy came toward them, whose menacing gaze seemed to condemn the most innocent actions. In fact, he had no sooner perceived the princess and Psiphismate than he believed that it was the rendezvous of a criminal intrigue, and without seeking to inform himself of the truth or the subject of their conversation, he had them seized and bound by a number of men who were following him and taken away like criminals. That man was named Zelopside.

As the princess and Psiphismate were being taken away, they encountered a woman with an ugly physiognomy, who asked Zelopside who the prisoners were that he was taking away.

"I don't know them," Zelopside replied, "but I found them together in this desert, and I'm convinced that their conduct was criminal; that's why I'm taking them away."

"That's well done," said the woman, whose name was Sycophante. "It's necessary to take them before Agnoïse and have them punished. I'll go, if you like, to make accusations against them." As she spoke she insinuated herself into the escort and walked with the others, still talking disadvantageously about the prisoners.

On the way, Sycophante encountered two women, her friends, one of whom was named Ponirge, the other Prodite, who joined her, making her great amities.

Agnoïse was then in a great hall where she gave audiences to petitioners sitting on a rich tribunal, accompanied by Prolidose, Antadise, Photonose and Coyphite, her counselors.

Syncophante presented Florine and Psiphismate to them, saying that they were criminals who had been found in a solitary and hidden place, holding secret commerce, to the scorn of the laws, modesty and decency, that she had been obliged to have them brought to the audience in order to have them judged, and that if

Agnoïse's tribunal did not make a public example of them it would be a means of crowning vice and giving an entrance to all kind of disasters.

Prodite and Ponirge approved the sentiments and the speech of Sycophante and said that, the individuals having committed the crimes of which Sycophante accused them, they merited, incontrovertibly, being severely judged.

Zelopside came forward in his turn and said that what Sycophante, Prodite and Ponirge had explained was just.

After having heard the accusations, Agnoïse got up from her seat and consulted opinions. As she sat down again in order to pronounce a rigorous sentence, Psiphismate, seeing that Florine and he were about to be condemned without being heard, raised his voice and asked for permission to explain himself. That was granted to him.

Psipihismate told them that while he was wandering, passing through the deserts of the marvelous labyrinth, he had encountered the lady who was accused with him, who was alone on one of the mountains of the desert; that curiosity had caused him to approach her and to ask her what reasons had led her there and what she was looking at with so much attention. The lady had responded to him that it was the desire to see and liberate Feliciane, and that she was admiring her palace, which appeared to be very beautiful; that she had a desire to go there but that it appeared to her to be impossible. As he had been attempting the same design or a long time, he had sat down next to the lady in order to talk to her about the means of reaching the palace; and while they were having that serious conversation, Zelopside, having seen them, had approached them, had had them tied up and brought in that state to the audience. He said that the lady and he were innocent of the crimes of which they were accused; that it was not sufficient to say that they were criminals, but necessary to prove it, and, the accusers not having done that, as they were obliged to do, the lady and he demanded to be released, as having been wrongly arrested.

Agnoïse conferred again with her counselors, Photonose and Antadise wanted Florine and Psiphismate to be condemned, in spite of his arguments, but Prolidose and Coryphite were of the contrary opinion, whereupon Agnoïse ordered that the accused by imprisoned and that judgment of the trial would be deferred until Sycophante and the others had proven the crimes of which they accused them.

Florine and Psiphismate were stripped over everything valuable they had; the ring that the prince had given Florine was taken from her; they were put in chains and taken to a long and frightful subterranean vault, where they were attached facing one another. It was a consolation of sorts for Florine, in that misfortune, at least to be able to hear Psiphismate speak,

Sycophante, seeing herself obliged to find witnesses to prove her accusation, asked Zelopside whether he could provide any. "No," said Zelopside, "I have nothing else against them except having found them conversing together in the desert."

"But you can see," said Sycophante, "that that isn't sufficient."

At that moment, Exapente arrived, who had come to tell them about a good turn that she had just done. As she was about to tell them the story, Sycophante said: "We have other things to do than listen to you. I've accused two people of having committed crimes, and

Agnoïse's tribunal wants me to prove what I say, which I anticipate that it won't be possible to do, and which might cause people to lose the confidence they have I what I said."

"I know what's required," said Exapente. "It's necessary to render you a service; I promise you that I'll do all I can."

Sycophante and Zelopside were charmed by Exapente's promises, and as they knew her, they flattered themselves that they would have satisfaction.

Exapente, with a sad and afflicted expression, went to find Florine in her prison. Approaching her, she said: "My princess, I can't tell you how much dolor I feel in seeing you in this deplorable state. I know that you're innocent of the crimes of which you're accused, and that it's nothing but the work of a frightful calumny. But console yourself; heaven won't permit them to find souls black enough to depose against you. Be persuaded that, your accusers being unable to put you to death publicly, you'll be held here under false pretexts to prove from day to day what they say against you, hoping that the rigor of your prison will take your life. My princess, you don't know the inviolable laws of this tribunal, which free all the criminals who are brought here and denounced when they confess the crimes of which they are accused before the accusers have been able to prove them. It's the only means of getting you out of this affair. Time is pressing, my dear princess, break your irons. I'm telling what I would do if I were in the unfortunate position that you're in."

Florine believed what Exapente said, to such an extent that she was disposed to make that confession, when Psiphismate, who had heard everything, said to her: "My princess, refrain from doing what this deceptive woman tells you; it's a trap that is being set for you in order to doom us. Princess, we are innocent of the crimes of which we're accused; heaven will take care of justifying us, and it would be an offense against it not to hope for that and to make a false confession in order to free us."

That speech astonished Exapente and caused her to withdraw. She went to find Sycophante and Zelopside to tell them about the failure of her journey. She told them that she had persuaded the lady to confess the crimes of which she was accused, but that the young man who was in prison with her had overturned everything in a moment; that while he was there and could advise her nothing could be achieved on the woman's mind; that they must see what could be done to shut the young man's mouth and that he would tempt other means of gaining her.

That news put the accusers in a bad mood; they went to consult Antadise and Photonose, to whom they repeated what Exapente had just told them, asking them what they could do to conserve their good reputation.

Hemotille was ordered to go into the prison in order to constrain Psiphismate, by means of all sorts of torments, to confess his crime. That was promptly executed, in such a violent manner that poor Psiphimate remained on the floor, only showing feeble signs of life.

The princess, who was a witness to so much cruelty, would have died in consequence if Hypomone had not sustained and fortified her, telling her that it was often futile and even bad to be afflicted and to want to oppose our pains to our enemies; that the best temperament one could bring to it was to suffer and to regard with tranquility the various movements of good and ill fortune; that it was quite usual to see one succeeded the other, and that, by that means, she could hope that things might change.[5]

At that moment two women came in, who approached Psiphismate, Florine asked them who they were and begged them to care for him.

"My name is Yssatie," said the first.

"And I'm Diagine," said the other. "He's a friend of ours and we've come to give him pleasure."

Immediately, Yssatie embraced Psiphismate and lifted him from the ground where he had fallen. Then Diagine made him take liquors that she had bought, which revived him.

Seeing Psiphimate recovered, Florine forgot, so to speak, the unfortunate state that she was in, and while she was expressing her gratitude to the ladies, she perceived a light at the entrance to the prison, which gave her a new terror, fearing that it was yet another misfortune that was about to overwhelm them. But how agreeably surprised she was when she perceived Probus, accompanied by two ladies!

As soon as she could be heard she said: "Oh, prince, you've come just in time to extract me from the state I'm in! But who told you about the need I had of you?"

"It was this beautiful lady you can see who told me about the evils that you were being made to suffer," said Probus, indicating one of the ladies who were accompa-

---

[5] The allegory of this episode is difficult to construe, in spite of the decoding obligingly provided by the editor's key to the meaning of the symbolic names. There is, however, an inevitable temptation to relate it to the condemnation of *contes de fées* as a result of slanderous rumors and the imprisonment of the Comtesse de Murat, their most influential writer.

nying him. "This lady is named Hallitie, and her companion is Dicayosine."

Florine expressed her gratitude to them for having rendered her such a great service, and was unable to weary of gazing at them, particularly Hallitie, who was so beautiful and splendid that the light emanating from her body illuminated the entire prison.

Then Dicayosine, having approached Florine, touched the irons by which she was enchained; they fell into dust, and the princess found herself free. Dicayosine did as much for Psiphismate, and the two prisoners did not know how to thank them for such great favors.

They were about to recommence making compliments to their liberators when the prince said to them: "Let's finish what is still to be done." He took the princess's hand, and they emerged from the prison.

As soon as Agnoïse, Sycophante and the other persecutors of the princess and Psiphismate saw Hallitie and Dicayosine, they fled in order to go and hide. The prince pursued them, and made them return the ring they had stolen from Florine. Then he took the princess to a plain, where he showed her the road she had to follow.

"You're going to abandon me again, then, my prince," said Florine.

"Not for long," he replied, "and you have your ring in order to warn me when you need me. Psiphismate is staying with you; he'll guide you well. You can have confidence in him; he's a faithful friend."

The prince having retired, Florine continued walking with Psiphismate.

Some time thereafter, Florine and Psiphismate arrived in a valley where there was a leafy boscage that seemed very agreeable to the princess. As she had just suffered considerably, the desire gripped her to go and rest there. She expressed her design to Psiphismate, who wanted to refuse, but for the sake of complaisance he went into the boscage with her.

The princess having sat down in the place that seemed most suitable, Psiphismate sat down next to her. They talked for a long time about the perils they had just avoided and the thanks that they gave to heaven for having delivered them from them. Gradually, the light breezes in the boscage lulled Florine to sleep. Seeing that she was asleep, Psiphismate tried to stay awake, but whatever efforts he made, he fell asleep too.

In that torpor, Florine thought that she was on a slippery slope, on the edge of a terrible precipice, and that dread was so violent for her that she woke up, paralyzed by fear. When she awoke she saw that she was not mistaken, and that the dream was only too true. She had no sooner opened her eyes than she saw that she was on the slope of a precipice, and whatever efforts she made to retreat from it, she could not succeed in doing so.

The poor princess called to Psiphismate several times for help, but in vain; he was profoundly asleep and did not hear her. Finally, the princess, making a great effort, took the ring from her bosom, and had no sooner put it in her mouth than Prince Probus arrived; he gave her his hand and put her back on the road that that she had quit.

The prince told Florine to continue her route without abandoning it, that she had seen the consequences of doing so, and he quit her again.

This time, the princess could not see the prince depart without a great sadness; she saw only too clearly the need she had of him. Having remarked the trouble that it caused her, the prince told her, in order to console her, that he was going to see Queen Feliciane to inform her of the design she had to release her from the labyrinth and to beg her to spare her the fatigues of the road.

Florine continued walking then, and Psiphismate caught up with her; she was overjoyed to see him again. He asked her how she had been able to escape from the peril she was in. "It was Prince Probus," said Florine, "who got me out of it. He came to me as soon as I put my ring in my mouth and put me back on the road. But tell me, my dear Psiphismate, what that boscage was that appears so charming, and why it is so pernicious to enter and repose there?"

Psiphimate replied that the boscage was named Amelite, and that it hid nonchalance and relaxation in its bosom.

As they continued talking they encountered on the road a woman of majestic bearing clad in white and brilliant cloth, who asked the princess if she was the person seeking Queen Feliciane.

"Yes, Madame," replied the princess. "I'm seeking that queen in order to release her from the labyrinth."

"Then it's you that I'm seeking too," said the lady. "Follow me and you'll soon have the good fortune of seeing her."

The lady was named Leucotisse; she was Feliciane's principal favorite.

"Our good queen has sent me to abridge your journey," she said, addressing Florine, "and I have orders to take you to her by the shortest route. All the terrain you see around us offers many perilous places through which you ought to pass, and where there would be reason to fear for you, but Prince Probus has begged the queen to anticipate you. Achakie and Pisonide have joined their plea to that of the prince, with the result that Feliciane has sent me to spare you the troubles that you still have to suffer."

A short time later they found themselves on the edge of a lake surrounded by tall trees; the lake had a small island in the middle, where the queen's palace was.

As soon as they perceived the palace, two women stepped into a boat and came to fetch them. Florine recognized them as Achakie and Pisonide, who gave their hand to the princess in order to help her into the boat and led her toward the queen, who came out of her palace to receive her.

As soon as Florine had set foot in that incomparable abode she was transported by joy and pleasure. The queen embraced her and gave her hand to her in order to conduct her into the palace.

While the princess respired the sweetness of a perfect tranquility, the queen gave orders, and when everything was ready, she set forth with Florine and the other women of her court.

The rumor ran around the Palace of Fays that Florine had found the queen, that they had set forth together and that they were traveling in long stages in order to return to the court.

That news afflicted Mauritianne, who sent her confidante to ascertain whether it was true. She reported that Feliciane and Florine were arriving rapidly. Mauriitanne immediately had equipages prepared, and quit the court in order to go to her islands with all her retinue.

The good fays who were awaiting impatiently for the return of Queen Feliciane and Florine went to meet them, and, having found them not far from the palace, as soon as they perceived them they uttered great cries of joy. The sage fay counselor was the first to approach the queen's chariot. Her love and her zeal for the queen and for Florine had caused her to go ahead of the others; Florine's good friend followed her, and when he fays arrived they all saluted the queen at once, while expressing to her the extreme joy they felt on her return. They arranged themselves before and after the chariot for their march and formed a reception procession worthy of their queen.

As they entered the grand courtyard of the palace nothing could be heard anywhere but acclamations and cries of delight, and several concerts singing the praises of the queen and the glory of Florine. It would not be easy to say here what the sentiments of the queen and the fays were on seeing themselves reunited again. Prince Probus was there, and the rest of the day was spent in the greatest rejoicing.

The next day, the queen and Florine mounted a golden chariot studded with precious stones. They went to the temple of Virtue, to which all the fays accompanied them. After great ceremonies in actions of grace for the fortunate return of the queen and Florine, Feliciane had a crown of inestimable price brought, which she took between her hands, and, turning toward the fays, she said to them:

"My dear sisters, you know why the supreme intelligences judged it appropriate to order me to quit my throne and render to the Marvelous Labyrinth until a mortal was found of excellent virtue who would have the strength to enter it, and overcome all the obstacles that opposed the means of finding me there. What do we not owe, then, my dear sisters, to this princess, who wanted to enter the labyrinth and, after having generously suffered there the fatigue of an infinity of labors and chagrins, finally reached me, and is the cause of me re-mounting the throne today? Thus, to testify to this princess a part of the recognition of the great obligations that we have to her, I believe it appropriate to crown her once again. She merits it."

As she pronounced these words, the queen placed the crown she was holding on Florine's head. In the meantime, all the fays sang praises in honor of Florine, to which concerts of all sorts of musical instruments responded.

Prince Probus could not contain the joy that he felt at seeing the princess crowned for a second time in the temple of Virtue. He had never seen her as beautiful as she appeared to him at her latest coronation. On returning from that assembly he went to see the princess in her apartment, to express the pleasure he had in all the honors that were being done to her. The fay counselor and her good friend did likewise.

While all these things were happening in the Palace of the Fays, Florine's father, the king, having vanquished his enemies, returned to the castle from which Florine had been abducted. As he approached that place his mourning was renewed for the loss of the princess. He had never been able to discover anything, whatever research he carried out, except that a thick cloud had enveloped her and that she had disappeared instantly.

Having arrived at the castle, the king sent for the magician, and asked him why he had deceived him in assuring him that he had rendered the castle inaccessible against any surprise and insult, for the conservation of the young princess he had left there, what had become of her, and if that was the effect of his promises.

"The princess is in good health," said the magician. "She overstepped the bounds that I had traced; she should return before long, and her abduction has been entirely glorious for her. A great prince will come to accompany her, to whom you ought to give the princess and to receive as your son-in-law.

Feliciane assembled her council, where it was agreed that Florine would be conducted to the king, her father, with all the marks of grandeur that were possible, not only because of her merit but also to repair the insult that had been done to her by having abducted her.

All the fays prepared to appear with splendor in that escort.

In the meantime, Probus was overwhelmed by sadness at the loss of the princess, whom he loved tenderly, and the sight of whom was his most cherished delight. He withdrew to a solitary place, where his heart could not help shedding tears, by virtue of an excess of amour and dolor.

As the prince was thinking about means of at least being able to reveal his extreme amour to the princess, Feliciane, who was walking in the palace gardens, surprised him in the arbor where he was, and had no sooner seen him than she said to him, laughing: "What, Prince! Are you the only person in the court who is not making dispositions to escort Florine to her father, in order to set the final seal on all her victories? You, in particular, have always taken so much care to lend her a hand in all the perils to which she might have succumbed!"

"Florine has no more need of my feeble aid," replied Probus. "She enjoys a solid felicity next to you; but if I could persuade myself that I might still be...."

The queen interrupted him. "It's necessary that you accompany the princess in her triumph. Time is pressing; quit this solitude and think about preparing yourself to augment the pompous equipage with which we intend to conduct her."

The prince obeyed the queen, and as lovers always flatter themselves, he thought he had seen in the manner in which the queen had spoken to him that she had penetrated the reason for his sadness and was thinking about means to render him happy with regard to the princess.

He was not mistaken. The queen had seen what had made Probus act in all the things he had done for the princess, and the sage fay counselor had revealed the passion that the prince had for her, so he was in a better position than he thought. He was almost within reach of the favorable moments that were to recompense him for all that he had done for Florine.

When everything was ready for the departure Feliciane quit her palace and set forth in good order. Four pompous chariots opened the march, in which there were as many musical concerts singing the praises of Florine. Those chariots were preceded and followed by a large quantity of fays, which responded by playing various musical instruments. Other fays followed them, carrying paintings in which Florine's victories were depicted. Prince Probus followed the paintings with a cortege of the most beautiful fays, magnificently dressed and crowned with laurels, myrtles and roses. The fay counselor and Florine's good friend followed the prince in superb chariots, carrying the princess's two crowns on rich cushions. Several fays accompanied those chariots, incessantly repeating, by means of cries of joy, that those crowns had been given to Florine to recompense her virtue. Simpliciane, Achakie, Pisonide and Leucotisse were in another chariot, making up a charming concert singing the praises of Florine's victory in the marvelous labyrinth. Then came Princess Florine, crowned with laurels, accompanied by Queen Feliciane, both in a gold and ivory chariot draw by eagles. The whole march was terminated by a host of richly adorned fays.

When that pompous assembly arrived in the king's lands, the rumor spread everywhere, and when the news reached Florine's father, he emerged from his palace in order to see what it could be.

At that moment two fays approached him. The king was surprised by the beauty and splendor of the two individuals and asked them what they wanted of him.

The fays replied: "Sire, Queen Feliciane asks you for permission to see you and to enter your palace with her entire court."

The king replied that he was very honored that the great queen wanted to do him the favor of entering his abode; that he would go to meet her in order to anticipate her and to have the honor of saluting her and welcoming her. The fays told him that he queen desired that he wait for her in his palace, and that she would arrive shortly.

The king, having reentered his palace, had his court assemble in order to receive Feliciane. Scarcely had his orders been carried out than the first ranks of the triumph were seen approaching, in admirable order.

On entering the palace, the procession arranged itself on both sides of the courtyard. The king, surprised to see such great magnificence, did not know what it signified, but when he saw the paintings of Florine's victories he began to believe that it was his daughter whom Queen Feliciane was bringing back to his palace. He looked for a long time at the prince, who was lined up like the others, but very close to the vestibule through which the apartments of the palace were entered, and the king remembered what the magician had said to him.

Finally, Feliciane's chariot arrived. As soon as he king saw it, he advanced to receive the queen, and was overjoyed when he recognized Florine beside her. He presented his hand to the queen to help her descend from her chariot, and Feliciane took Florine's. The three of them went together to the most beautiful apartment in the palace.

Feliciane presented Florine to the king, her father, saying: "Sire, here is the princess you thought you had lost; she has had many chagrins, and has been exposed to many perils, but they have only served to raise her to a higher degree of honor and glory. The crowns you see are the prize of victories that she has acquired with the aid of Prince Probus, whom I introduce to you."

The king embraced the prince, with sentiments of gratitude, and Feliciane, continuing her discourse, begged the king to receive him in his alliance, and to recompense him also by giving him the princess, his daughter, whom he loved more than himself.

"Madame," said the king, "the choice is glorious for my daughter and myself, since it comes from you; it is very little for such a generous prince, to whom we have such great obligation. I would like to have several crowns to present to him as well as my daughter; I would think myself to happy if he would do me the honor of receiving them and accepting them."

The prince testified a part of his gratitude to the king and Queen Feliciane; and Florine, having heard mention of marrying the prince, had an inconceivable joy in consequence; gratitude for the generosity he had

had for her gave birth at that moment in her heart for a violent amour for the prince.

The rumor of the marriage spread everywhere; everyone prepared for the great ceremony, which was celebrated with all possible magnificence. Afterwards, Queen Feliciane retired with her court to her estates, and the prince remained with the princess.

BOCA; or, VIRTUE RECOMPENSED

In Lima, the capital of Peru, there was a man in whom intelligence and good looks were a gift of simple nature. His education had been proportionate to the mediocrity of his estate. He was the son of a sculptor; his father had enjoyed a rather considerable fortune for a man of his profession, but misfortunes had almost reduced him to poverty, and young Boca, his son, was born in the time of his misfortune. His mother, who died giving birth to him, only left the fruit of their marriage to her husband for a consolation.

The boy was brought up to handle a chisel, but as a few small funds are required in order to have marble materials or choice stone, which were necessary to him, he saw himself constrained to degenerate by reducing himself to carpentry work. He became skillful enough to hope the work would one day enable him to subsist honestly. His father also ended his life, satisfied to leave in his son a man who, in spite of his youth, did not seem to have any inclination to vice, and who, by virtue of sentiments more delicate and more elevated than those of his peers usually are, encouraged the belief that he loved virtue.

Young Boca, after having given some time to his grief, finding the talent for polishing and perfecting that which emerged from his hands, applied himself particularly to turning ivory. He succeeded in that perfectly, but as those sorts of works are not among those that enter into the utility of life, it was rare that he sold them, so that was not his ordinary work; he only devoted two hours a day to it, which he stole more often than not from his slumber.

One day he was in his shop when a man came in to ask him whether he had any boxes. Boca showed him one that he had finished the day before. The man found it good enough, and gave him six piastres for it without bargaining.

At the sight of that sum, Boca thought that his probity was being tempted, and said to the stranger: "If I took what you are offering, do you think that I would be an honest man? This is the work of six hours, and I ought not to receive such a large price; if you don't know that, it's up to me to tell you; and if you do know it, learn what I am."

The stranger smiled, and after adding a further six piastres to those he had counted out, he said: "My friend, is it not liberal and laudable to make gifts? Take from this sum what is due to you, and receive the rest as a present."

He withdrew immediately.

Boca was surprised and charmed to possess without reproach a sum so large by comparison with what such works usually produced. *Alas*, he said to himself, *that my poor father is not still alive. What joy he would have in seeing me so well paid for such scant trouble. What a pleasure it would be for me to share this good fortune with him.*

Then, taking his money, he went to put it in a small coffer and, giving thanks to the gods, he returned to his work more cheerfully than usual.

A few days later, he merchants who sold him ivory, passing his door, asked him whether he wanted to buy any.

"Gladly," he said. After having made his choice, he asked them to wait while he went to fetch the money with which to pay them. He ran to his coffer, but after having opened it, he was surprise to see that there was no longer any money in it, only a quantity of ants. Consternated, he went downstairs, and in order to smooth things over with the merchants he made them understand that he had believed he had enough to satisfy them but that he was mistaken; he asked for a delay of a month.

When they had gone, his first concern was to wonder how it was possible that he had been robbed, seeing no appearance of it, since the coffer had been securely locked and he had not told anyone about his adventure.

As he was thinking about it sadly he heard his name called, and on looking up he saw a richly dressed man, who bowed to him.

"Boca," the man said to him, "do you have an ivory box?"

"Alas, Sire," he replied, "I wish to heaven that I had never made any. I would not be experiencing mortal chagrin at present. I was well paid a few days ago for one that I sold, and by an unparalleled generosity, the man who bought it gave me twelve piastres, but either they have been stolen from me or the gods want to afflict me; I no longer found them were I had put them, and it would have been better for me if I had never felt the pleasure of possessing them.

"That loss is not irreparable," said the man. "Go find me a box and you'll recover your money."

Boca ran to do that, and after showing him one, the man immediately counted out twenty-four piastres.

Boca thought he was dreaming; motionless, his eyes fixed on the piastres, he could not get over his astonishment. Gratitude was about to make him fall at his bene-factor's knees, but he perceived that he had gone.

"Whoever you are, generous stranger," he ex-claimed, "may fortune render you a thousand times more than you have given me."

Transported by joy, he picked up his money, exam-ined it, counted it, recounted it, and, still astonished, locked it in another coffer, more solidly and exactly locked than the first.

He was already disposing of that small treasure, and, believing that he would be able to buy everything he needed, he thought about paying his debts, dressing more properly, regaling his friends, and even making them little presents, without perceiving that twenty times as much would not be sufficient to fulfill his projects. Coming to his senses, however, he perceived that a part of the day had gone by without him having put his hand to work.

"Come on, Boca," he said, "don't let good fortune make you fall into idleness. Your father was once richer than you; let the example of his misfortunes teach you that fortune is inconstant; seek to sustain yourself by your toil."

The rest of the day was spent turning boxes similar to the first; he took so much pleasure in it that they were masterpieces of their species.

Before going to bed, he was seized by a desire to see his new treasure again. He went to the coffer, but having opened it he was prevented from seeing but a cloud of flies that emerged from it in great numbers. But, frightful despair, no more piastres: there were only in-sects inside!

It is not possible to describe that state Boca was in at that sight. He scarcely had strength enough left to feel his wore.

"Oh, cruel and detestable magician," he cried—for all that he had heard said about fays and genii suddenly returned to his memory, and he attributed his misfortune to some charm—"what have I done to experience your malice? Why make me savor so much pleasure, if I must always be misfortunate? Have I asked you to make me gifts? I didn't know the dolor that I'm feeling."

A few tears escaped him as he pronounced the last words, and after having thought for some time about his misfortune, he went on: "My father, you were a man of honor and you had more to lament than me; I've seen you support reverses even more frightful with courage, why should I have fewer than you?"

That reflection calmed him down, and, taking the scraper in hand, he returned to work, and sent part of the night in it.

In the following days he applied himself even more assiduously than usual, and scarcely obtained two hours sleep a night. Chagrin, fatigue and the anxiety caused to him by the debt he had contracted to the ivory merchants, which came back to mind incessantly, caused him to fall dangerously ill. He was assisted by neighbors who liked him, and their generous cares succeeded. He had not confided his troubles to anyone, but he soon found himself obliged to make them known.

On the sixth day of his illness, finding himself much better, he asked the people taking care of him to help him to go down into his shop, in order to arrange, he said, for some commissioned work that it was necessary to deliver, for which he needed to receive the price.

When he had done that, a rather aged man of respectable appearance came in holding in his hand the box for which Boca had received twenty-four piastres and said to him: "Do you have a box like this one?"

At that sight, Boca felt all his anger reborn, and, in spite of his weakness, he seized the old man by the arm. "My friends," he said to the people who were with him, "Help me to punish an impostor and a rogue; he has deceived me wickedly, by dazzling me with imaginary treasures, and withheld the meager salary that is due to me for the boxes I have delivered to him."

They listened without being able to understand what he was saying, but the old man was unmoved. "I make you judges in this affair," he said to them. "This man, I believe, has lost his mind. He has never seen me before and is demanding without reason for I know not what money, which I do not owe him."

"I've never seen him before, it's true," said Boca, "but was that box not made by me?"

"I don't know," said the old man "All that I know is that it belongs to me; if someone has stolen it from you, is it for me to answer for it? I would like, however, to render its value to you, in order to repair the fault that a dishonest man might have committed against you."

Boca found himself confounded by that speech, and, his friends having applauded and praised the old man, the latter asked for a box similar to the one that he was showing. He was brought the six most recently made. He chose one, with which he seemed very content. Then, taking out a long purse that he had in his belt, he laid out fifty piastres on the workbench.

At the sight of that sum, the spectators opened their eyes wide without proffering a word, but Boca cried: "No, no, keep your money; I don't want it. I won't be caught again, I'm not as stupid as you think. Truly, it's easy for you to give away such money. My box will always be a box, but your money will probably only produce moths."

At that speech, no one doubted that the poor man had lost his mind; they argued with him, and tried to make him listen to reason, but he did not want to be moved.

"I need six reals," he cried, and I don't want any more. Piastres bring me bad luck."

They tried to interrogate him, but he did not want to hear anything. Voices were raised, and they all treated him as an insensate.

During that dispute, the old man left the fifty piastres and withdrew. Boca, who saw him leave precipitately, started crying: "Stop, thief!" and tried to run after him, but the door was closed and in spite of his resistance he was carried to his room and put to bed. They even deliberated as to what remedies to give him in order to bring him to his senses.

Those discourses having seemingly calmed him down, he made a sign that he wanted to speak, and they fell silent.

"My friends," he said, "I confess that I allowed my resentment to carry me away too heatedly, and that it was necessary to explain to you what quarrel I thought I had with that old man. But since he has escaped, listen to what has happened to me."

Then he told them the story of his adventures. Some of them had difficulty believing him; other still believed in the supernatural. It was concluded that someone would take the money to a changer, to verify whether it was honest coin

The money-changer assured them that it was impossible to find better piastres, and Boca, slightly reassured, locked them in a third coffer in the presence of the witnesses, who all swore that they had seen them, after which they retired and wished him god night.

Poor Boca reflected on that last adventure for a long time; he dared not yield to the joy of having so much wealth; a surge of anxiety made him get up and go to the coffer. *Let's see them one more time*, he said to himself; but then he stopped and went back to bed. *No*, he continued; *let's go to sleep rich again this time*. Shortly afterwards he fell asleep.

Early in the morning the next day he heard knocking on the door of his shop. It was the merchants. He asked them to wait for a moment, and approached the coffer that contained his treasure, tremulously. He opened it with a black presentiment that was only to well-founded. "Just gods," he cried, no longer seeing the piastres, "What will become of me?" Then, letting himself fall into a chair next to the coffer, he stayed there for a long time, bewildered and motionless.

The merchants, who became impatient, went up to his room and found him in that condition. One of them nudged his arm. "Come on, Boca, what are you dreaming about? We're in a hurry. We're leaving tomorrow for Guinea, we can't stop any longer."

Turning his sad eyes toward them, Boca said: "Do with my whatever you please, my friends. I'll submit to anything; dispose of my life, I'll lose it without regret."

They did not understand what he was saying.

Showing them the coffer, he went on: "Yesterday, there were fifty piastres in this coffer, and I no longer find them there. Don't think that it's a deceit I'm attempting in order not to pay you, I still have a little money, my furniture, my tools and a part of the ivory you sold me; take from all that whatever you think appropriate."

He seemed so distraught in pronouncing those words that the sighs accompanying them touched the most considerable among them; he had understood that Boca had been robbed, and without asking for further clarification he said,: "Well, Boca, where's the rest of the ivory? Go fetch it."

It was represented to him immediately, and, having calculated the amount that had been used, the man said: "It's necessary that those to whom Fortune is favorable acquit themselves toward her by repairing the harm she does to the unfortunate. What you've used in approximately the sum that we've gained with you; it's just to return it to you. I offer to indemnify those of us who don't want to consent to that. As for the rest of the ivory, that reverts to us, I'll give you my share in order to leave you in a condition to continue your labor."

The others followed such a generous example, and Boca threw himself at their feet, shedding tears of affection and gratitude, and rendering them a thousand thanks.

The merchants withdrew, and Boca thought himself the happiest man in the world; his joy had never been so keen. He counted the past for nothing. The coffer, which was still open, was put with the other two in a corner of his shop, in order to be broken up as soon as possible, so that he would no longer see objects that had caused him so much chagrin. As he was arranging them, however, he heard something moving inside.

Looking immediately, in order to see what it might be, he found a small ebony road a foot long, both ends of which were armed with a highly polished metal brilliant in color, similar to gold. He picked it up, and tried to close the coffer, but in vain; it always opened again of its own accord.

Quickly, he went to the other two. Lifting the lid of the first, he saw inside large shell similar to the cocoon of a silkworm. As the lid of the coffer was raised, the shell opened, and when it had done so completely, he saw a bird of marvelous beauty emerge. Its head was the color of flame, its neck white, its wings yellow, the underside and upper part of its body gray. Its tail violet and its feet black.

The bird looked at him as of it wanted to speak to him, but Boca was only intent on considering its plumage. He soon saw it take flight and alight in a corner of the room. As he followed it with his eyes he perceived a monstrous spider, which pounced on it instantly. The bird uttered a cry, and they both disappeared.

What new prodigy is this? What does it mean? he said to himself. *Should I call my neighbors, in order to recount these marvels to them? No, they'd think I'm insane; it's better to see what becomes if it all. I'm well; I have what I need to work, let's go on as usual. If the metal at the end of my stick is gold, it'll still be worth something.*

He took it out of his pocket in order to examine it more closely. At the bottom he felt silver coins: there were four reals.

Good, he went on. *That's not bad; if I could find as many every day, I wouldn't ask for anything more. But for fear that what happened to the piastres might happen to them, let's take advantage of them.*

He went out to buy food, and came back quite content to turn his ivory.

The next day, rummaging in his pocket, he found another four reals. Determined to test whether it was his little stick that was lavishing that marvelous income on him, when he went to bed, he laid it down in the coffer in which he had found it.

When he woke up, he only found in the coffer, with his stick, a piece of paper on which these words were written:

> *Without embarrassing yourself for the journey,*
> *Go to the Orient; arm yourself with courage,*
> *Do not stop on the way,*
> *However many obstacles you find;*
> *Boca, in order to work miracles*
> *It is sufficient to be humane.*
> *If you obey this supreme order,*
> *An entire people will owe you happiness;*
> *You will become happy yourself.*
> *Depart, for fear arriving at the extreme of misfortune.*

He hesitated for some time to make his resolution, but finally, flattering himself that all the marvels he had seen must have a goal advantageous to his fortune, he closed his shop, and went to inform himself as to which road it was necessary to take to go to the Orient. He did so in such a fashion that no one suspected his design. He learned that a ship was ready to set sail for the island of Java.[6]

---

[6] If one starts from Peru, one travels westwards to reach Java rather than eastwards, but place names seem to be used in the story arbitrarily, and it is profoundly unclear how the main

As he wanted to obey exactly the order that had been prescribed to him not to stop on the way, he went to see the captain of the ship, in order to ask whether he would be staying long on that island. He knew that the majority of those embarking were going there to buy rice, but there were a few pillagers who counted on setting sail again immediately for Japan. Boca told the captain that he would go with the latter party, that the route in question was the one he wanted to follow. Then they came to an arrangement, and he was told to be in the port in three days.

Having returned home, he hastened to sell a substantial part of anything that could procure him some money. He reread his piece of paper several times a day, and his faithful little stick, when it was in his pocket, always produced four reals, so he was careful to leave it there.

When the three days had expired, he went to the port and embarked. The navigation was fortunate, and not long after, they arrived in Java at daybreak. Immediately, Boca, thinking about the order that instructed him not to stop, asked whether the ship that was to take him to Japan was ready to depart. He learned to his chagrin that it would not be ready to set sail for a fortnight, and that all those in port at the time would be taking an opposite direction.

That news had an effect on him that astonished him. *Why*, he said to himself, while walking along the shore, *do I feel struck with dread and displeasure at this delay? Why do I find myself subjugated by a chimerical com-*

---

locations in which the story is set correspond to locations on the globe.

mand? Where am I going? And whence comes the de-termination to follow a route unknown to me, with no other goal than to obey a note found by chance in a cof-fer, a note which might perhaps signify nothing, which the malice of one of my enemies might have caused me to find there in order to test my credulity? However, he continued, *the prodigies that I am quite sure of having seen, and the one my little stick operates, mark some-thing supernatural in my adventures. I even sense that it would be very difficult to resist it. My destiny orders it; it's necessary to follow the order.*

He was extracted from that reverie by the cry of a bird that landed at his feet; it was similar to the one he had seen emerge from the coffer in his bedroom. Piqued by curiosity, and hoping, if he could catch it, to possess something rare and marvelous, he tried to seize it, but the bird flew away lightly and stopped twenty paces away from him. Boca ran after it, and believed that he had it when it took off again and flew further. Piqued by the adventure, Boca pursued it, and, never losing sight of it, always ran after it.

A good part of the day passed in that exercise. Fi-nally weary and fatigued, he was ready to abandon the enterprise when he noticed that the bird was itself hardly able to fly any longer. In fact, with one last effort it launched itself into a small boat that was stationary on the sea shore, and appeared to fall there, as if dead. Without making any reflection, Boca jumped into the boat, and, searching with his eyes for the place where it had fallen, he saw it flying over the deck. At the same time, the little vessel departed, and drew away from the port with extreme velocity.

Seized by fear, he raised his eyes skywards, and perceived the mast of a ship, covered with birds like the one he had just pursued, which were uttering piercing cries and flapping their wings as if to testify their joy. His surprise was unimaginable; it increased even further when he saw that he was alone, having no company but that of insects of several species.

He remarked among them an intelligence that did not make them useless. Applying himself to consider more exactly what was happening between them, he recognized that the birds were carrying out maneuvers, and that one of them was serving as pilot. That was not all; the sails were made of spider-webs, and the rigging was so delicate that he judged it to be the same fabric. The boat was so small that no similar one had ever been constructed; everything was proportioned with an admirable accuracy.

Having entered the poop cabin he found it carpeted with a rush mat so delicately wrought that from a distance of a few feet one might have mistaken it for the finest Genoa satin; in the middle of each piece the word *Orient* was inscribed in relief in colored wax. As he scanned all those inscriptions he perceived that the coloration of one word was not finished, but a large number of flies had settled thereon, and they were toiling with an admirable industry to complete their work. Some were disgorging a green liquid over the wax, others were dragging butterfly wings with their feet, painting the characters so distinctly, and with so much artistry, that a painter's brush could not have done better.

Boca was considering all these things with admiration when another spectacle was offered to his eyes. In one of the corners of the cabin a large quantity of ants was extending over the floor a mat three feet square, and others were carrying a block of wax filled with honey, which they placed in the middle. The ants left the room then, but returned soon afterwards pushing small pine-apples before them, which they arranged on the mat in an orderly manner. Several approached Boca, seemingly inviting him to partake of the meal. He consented to do that, and after having tasted the honey, which seemed to him to be exquisite, he opened one of the fruits, and slaked his thirst with the delicious liquid inside.

After that frugal meal, wanting to content his curi-osity, he followed the ants, which carried what remained out of the cabin. He went through an extremely low door into a small space where he saw a large number of the animals in question, occupied in several tasks. Six tiny barrels were open; the first two were full of fresh water, the others filled with grain, midges, pineapples and sticks of wax. His pleasure was not mediocre on seeing his little vessel so well provisioned.

The sun was about to set, and the little boat, which seemed to be flying over the waves with the aid of a light breeze, had already covered a considerable distance when he went up from the poop cabin. He found a bed set up in a form similar to that of the hammocks that are ordinarily employed on ships; it was a mat suspended by cords wrought by spiders, and a feather-bed, the quilt of which resembled the finest muslin. It was only raised up three feet, but that was enough for him not to want to risk falling out of it, so Boca tugged it rudely, wanting to lay it on the deck, but the prodigious quantity of the little cords resisted his efforts.

"O gods," he cried, "how little the weak ought to be scorned, and how powerful they are, on the contrary, when they are united by order and industry!"

He tried again, several times, to bring it down, but in vain, which obliged him to lie down in it with confi-dence, not without having read his piece of paper and looked at his little stick again, which was still accompanied by four reals.

He did not sleep much that night, but only reflected on his enterprise and everything admirable he had seen. What worried him was not knowing how long he would spend in this state, deprived of commerce with humans and exposed to the dangers of the sea. Those afflicting thoughts dissipated with the shadows of the night, and the commencement of a beautiful day restored calm in his soul.

That day passed like the first, and when night fell he was recompensed by a gentle slumber for the agitations of the previous one.

On the fourth day of navigation he was woken up before dawn by the piercing cries of the birds and the buzzing of the flies. That noise alarmed him. He went up on deck and found a considerable part of the inhabitants of the little vessel there. He judged by their movements that something extraordinary was happening. However, the serene atmosphere and the tranquil waves were already reassuring him with regard to his fear when even shriller and sadder cries succeeded the first; disorder was manifest in those carrying out the maneuvers; the helm was abandoned and all the animals precipitated themselves *en masse* into the hold.

The object of that scare seemed to be a small cloud that was forming; and looking up, he saw it grow rapidly, open up and emit lightning bolts that seemed to have no other objective than the destruction of his feeble retreat, Courageous and submissive, he prayed to the gods for help, but a powerful protection had anticipated his prayers; the thunderbolts did not reach their target; an invisible force repelled them violently, and sent them far away to fall uselessly into the waves.

The tempest dissipated, but he soon found himself exposed to another danger, which the commencement of nocturnal darkness rendered more frightful. A hundred fiery globes appeared to be rolling over the waves, and coming impetuously to set the vessel ablaze; but they were all stopped by mountains of water that rose up from the depths of the sea, falling back over the flames and swallowing them up in the sea.

Those two elements battled for a long time, but in the end, all the fires disappeared, and nothing remained but a thick black smoke, the pestilential odor of which would infallibly have made him perish if a whirlwind had not dissipated it promptly and returned the atmosphere to its original serenity.

They were still sailing at a prodigious velocity; all the animals resumed their ordinary posts, and Boca retired to his cabin, consigning his life to the care of the power that had saved him from an almost inevitable death by means of its prodigies. He found his meal served, and after having eaten it, he slept for a few hours.

The sun was already over the horizon when cries very similar to those of the previous day struck his ears again. He shivered, and dared not go to discover their cause.

He was still in that irresolution when he saw some of the various animals come into the cabin, which approached him precipitately, then returned to the door, and then came back to him, seemingly engaging him to follow hem, which he did. Scarcely had he come out when the vessel ran aground and stopped.

His joy was extreme at the sight of the most beautiful country in the world, and he flattered himself that his adventures would soon reach a fortunate conclusion. His little traveling companions all hastened to quit the vessel; the birds and the flies flew away into the nearby meadows; the ants and spiders dispersed here and there; and in a matter of moments he lost his little company— not without regret, for he was a man of habitude, he had received services from them, and had never been contradicted by them.

Having descended to the shore, he took the route that presented itself. When he had taken a few steps, a loud noise that he heard behind him obliged him to turn round; it was to see his little boat sink into the sea. That loss, combined with that of his traveling companions, wrung a sigh from him.

"Alas," he said, "that little retreat was pleasant, but I was burning with the desire to quit it; I quit it, and I regret it; has hope, then, anything so sweet? Flattered by its promises, it amuses us, and often draws us to our doom by multiplying our desires."

He was walking in a delightful meadow dotted with flowers, and his reflections were succeeded by admiration of the beautiful place. The pastureland was intercut by several streams, where a pure, clear water flowed over pebbles of various colors. A chain of mountains limited it to the north; charming landscapes extended to the west as far as the eye could see, and a dense forest terminated it to the east. He went into it by a beautiful wide road that was intersected at a distance of a hundred meters by others that were not as broad.

Exact in what had been prescribed by his oracle, Boca was marching on, resolute in not stopping, when he heard someone calling him, and saw an aged man nearby, who held out his hand to him.

"Stop a moment, friend," he said, "I have need of you."

As Boca kept walking, the man followed him.

"It's fortunate for you," he said, "to encounter me here; do you want to doom me by refusing me the help I'm requesting? The place from which you're drawing way contains a rich treasure, of which we can both be the possessors. I haven't confided my secret to anyone, and I hoped to be able on my own, having dug through six feet of earth, to lift up a stone that seals a small cavern where immense sums in gold and precious stones are contained. I've done what I can to carry it through, but, my great age having exhausted my strength, my efforts have been futile, and the hazard that brought you here causes me to believe that the gods want to associate themselves with my good fortune."

The old man having stopped speaking, Boca, who was examining him attentively, admired his respectable appearance, but the desire to yield to his discourse was violently combated by the dread of disobedience. Finally, making his decision generously, he replied "Whoever you are, don't hope or any help from me; I have scant obligation to you for the offer your making me; I owe it to your weakness. In any case, I can't approve of the desire you've conceived to possess immense riches that you cannot enjoy for long. I've learned from experience that Fortune deceives us in giving us more than we merit and that her excessive favors are sometimes the effect of her hatred. For myself, I don't want anything more than what I possess."

After this speech, the old man, not being put off, made further pleas, but when he saw that he could not attain his ends by persuasion, reproaches and imprecations escaped him.

"Go, villain," he said. "May the gods confound you, and may you find death where you footsteps are hastening." Immediately, he plunged into the densest part of the forest, and Boca lost sight of him.

A few paces further on he perceived an old woman curbed over the ground, who seemed to be looking for something in the bracken. When he was close enough to be heard, he said: "My good woman, tell me, I beg you, in what country I am."

The old woman, raising her head and staring at him, bowed to him without responding and resumed searching. Imagining that she had not heard, and finding himself quite close to her, Boca slowed his pace slightly and cried: "Good woman, tell me. I beg you, in what country I am, and whether I might find some retreat nearby."

"Eh?" said the old woman, lowering her head and looking at him shiftily. "Don't tell me you've found my spectacles? I lost them on this road—give them back to me."

Frowning, Boca raised his shoulders and his voice. "I'm asking you whether there's a retreat nearby, either a town or a village, and what country I'm in."

"Since you don't have my spectacles," she said, coldly, "let me search for them. I don't have time to tell you all that; when I have them, fine; if you're so curious, help me look for them and perhaps I'll reply to you."

He consented to that, not without some movements of impatience, and, walking slowly, both bent over, they searched very carefully. Sometimes, the old woman stopped, but Boca kept moving, slowly. Finally, the wretched spectacles were spotted by the old woman, who shouted to Boca: "I have them!" Then sitting down on the grass she gestured to him to do the same. "Let's rest and chat now," she said. "I'll tell you fine things."

Boca did not want to do that. "What?" he said. "You don't want to go on a little further, very gently?"

"I wouldn't get up from here for a kingdom," said the old woman. "I can't do any more, I'm so tired."

Raising his eyes to the heavens, and darting an indignant glance at her, Boca drew away from her, hastening his steps in fear of succumbing to the curiosity by which he was urgently pressed.

What! he said to himself, taking the piece of paper from his pocket and rereading it attentively. *What can the reason by for this letter demanding that I pursue my route without stopping for a moment? To what fatigue will I expose myself if I follow that order with scrupulous exactitude? Do the gods ever demand of people more than they can deliver? However, it tells me to overcome obstacles, and what shall I do if I don't reach the terminus of my hopes? A moment of weakness might cause me to lose the fruit of all that I've done thus far. Come on, let's have nothing for which to reproach ourselves.*

He had been walking for a quarter of an hour, his mind occupied by those thoughts, when he saw something white extended on the ground a little way in front of him. As he got closer he distinguished a small form of which he could not yet make out the features, but, having increased his pace, he saw a sheet laid on the ground. A young child as beautiful as the day was covering it with dishes very capable of inciting his desire; there was everything that a rich man in Lima would have been able to serve himself.

That sight revived his appetite, and the amiable child, coming to meet him, said: "Will you come and take a little refreshment? People who are interested in you have sent me in order to offer you this relief in order for you to recover your strength. Come and sit down and eat."

"Sit down?" retorted Boca.

"Of course," said the child. "You'll be more comfortable."

"I won't have anything," he replied.

Then, taking a loaf of bread in one hand, and a bottle and a slice of meat in the other, he continued walking. But the child blocked his path.

"You can't think so," he said. "Come and sit down with me on the grass to eat, or what you take will be useless to you." Then he blew on what Boca thought he was really holding, and everything vanished from his hands,

That prodigy afflicted him, but did not shake him On the contrary, applauding himself for not having fallen into the trap, he continued on his way, reflecting on the seductive chimeras by which almost all men would have allowed themselves to be drawn.

He had been walking for about four hours without turning off the highway when dolorous cries penetrated him all the way to the heart, causing him an extraordinary emotion. the further he went, he louder the cries became.

How frightened he was when he saw two men finishing tying a woman to a tree. Then, a surge of pity more powerful than dread caused him to forget that he had no weapon and that he was defenseless. He ran to her ardently, and seeing the cruel men draw their sabers in order to strike the unfortunate woman, he shouted: "Stop! Stop, inhuman barbarians!"

At those words, the men launched terrible gazes. "Be our first victim," they said. "Die, wretch!"

As soon as they raised their arms in order to immolate him to their fury, they both remained motionless, and it would not have taken much for Boca to resemble them, as he awaited the blow ready to fall on his head. Reassured, however, by the prodigy that had just protected his days, he felt his fear succeeded by a mortal displeasure. He had just stopped.

"I'm doomed!" he cried. "What have I done, fool!" Then, turning his eyes toward the object of his disobedience, he saw a young and charming woman who was smiling at him.

When he had come closer, she said to him: "Don't worry, Boca, have no fear that the action you've just performed will be imputed to you as a crime; is it not prescribed to be humane? Untie me and follow me; you have yet to undergo your final trial, but I will guide you, and henceforth you need not fear stopping."

At those words Boca sensed a secret movement of joy and confidence; the beautiful individual seemed to him to be a helpful goddess, on whom his destiny depended. He obeyed her, and the amiable stranger, having taken him by the hand, made him traverse several roads, from which they entered into another, fairly spacious one, but which narrowed as they advanced.

The trees, which were tightly packed and bushy, formed an arbor not only impenetrable to the sun's rays but almost inaccessible to daylight. Gradually, that faint light diminished, and the trees became lower and lower, forming a vault so obscure that it was scarcely possible to see in order to makes one's way.

Boca and his guide, still holding hands, walked without daring to talk. Anxiety, dread and the horror of that solitude caused him an agitation and a fear that chilled all his senses. It was further redoubled by the total suppression of the remaining light and the howling and frightful bellowing that he heard as soon as he ceased to be able to distinguish objects.

He imagined that he would doubtless soon fall prey to ferocious beasts; squeezing the hand of his guide more forcefully, he allowed himself to be dragged along like a criminal who, unable to avoid death, waits impatiently for the blow that will deliver him from the horrors that precede it.

They marched for quite a long time in that frightful darkness, and poor Boca, whose strength was exhausted, no longer able to resist such a violent situation, collapsed unconscious.

What was his surprise, however, when coming round, he found his strength reestablished and that place of horror changed into a magnificent garden ornamented with the most beautiful flowers, which, in exhaling their delicious perfumes into the air, completed making it an enchanted abode.

A confused noise of birds fluttering in bushes a few paces away caused him to turn his head in that direction. He saw with extreme pleasure that they were similar to those that had guided him in his navigation; that seemed to be a good augury, and hope was reanimated in his heart. He stood up, curious to study all the beauties offered to his eyes.

No longer seeing the amiable stranger who had guided him in the forest, he had no doubt that she was the one who had transported him to this place. Intent on searching for her, he traversed a flower garden in which all human artistry seemed to be exhausted, and nature surpassed herself. At the far end of the flower garden stood a palace of singular construction, ornamented with all the riches of the most superb architecture. Three kinds of marble formed the main body of the building; the top stratum was white, the middle black and the bottom a particular kind veined by several colors. The doors and windows were closed, and the silence that reigned everywhere made him think that the palace was uninhabited. However, everything in the garden was cultivated.

Two large groves of trees extended to the right and the left; one consisted of myrtles of an extraordinary height, the other of orange trees of a similar grandeur. Boca went into the former and saw a large oval of grass in the middle, on which a prodigious quantity of bee-hives, painted in various colors and symmetrically arranged, formed a very agreeable aspect. Twelve avenues of flowering myrtles lead to that arena; several palisades of interlaced jasmines and rose-bushes closed it around the perimeter, only interrupted by the openings of the avenues. In the middle of each palisade stood a grotto of rock and shells, from depths of which emerged a sheet of water, which fell rapidly into a marble basin of three colors, and then extended in various channels in order to irrigate the beautiful place.

After having admired that charming retreat, Boca went to slake his thirst at one of those fountains, and then went on his way.

On emerging from the grove he found himself in a small cypress wood. Those sad trees formed a melancholy shade; the arid ground only produced brambles and the sun only seemed to illuminate the wood regretfully, only lending a faint light to it.

Boca wanted to escape, but having already advanced too far, the paths that he took in order to emerge took him further forward. Finally, he perceived a small dome-shaped building, also in marble of three colors, from which light smoke was emerging.

What! he said to himself. *Is it possible that this dismal solitude is inhabited, while the charming places I have just seen are deserted?*

As he advanced in that direction, he saw a marble statue placed on a pedestal, which represented a woman sitting on a small throne, her legs folded and her head supported by one of her hands, in the posture of a person thinking deeply. She had a white head, a black body and legs of veined marble. She was so extraordinarily beautiful that Boca was transported by admiration, and struck by the excellence of the chisel-work.

"Who can have produced this masterpiece of art?" he exclaimed. "What divine hand has formed this marvel?" Then, addressing the statue as if it could hear him, he said: "You ought to ornament the most beautiful palace in the world. Who placed you in this frightful solitude?"

"Hatred and jealousy," replied the statue.

Boca recoiled three paces, seized by fear and astonishment. He had difficulty believing what he had just heard, Recovering somewhat from his disturbance, he wanted to interrogate the statue again, in order to clarify the matter.

"O gods!" he said "Is it possible that it was you who spoke to me? And...."

"Yes," the statue replied, interrupting him. "But don't worry, Boca; you can, if you wish, by destroying the charm that renders me the most unfortunate of princesses, become the most fortunate man in the world. This body you see contains a rational soul, in whom all the faculties have remained as the gods gave them to her, and the metamorphosis of my body, by an extraordinary prodigy, has not altered my senses and leaves me the liberty of my organs. My fate is all the more frightful because, although transformed into cold and inanimate matter, I bear a heart torn by dolor. However, the sight of you renders me hope, and your presence announces an imminent good fortune to me. You have overcome obstacles in order to get this far; now you must work miracles; it will be sufficient for you to be humane. You have already saved a woman from a terrible danger; finish what your courage has commenced."

These last words confounded Boca. "How is it possible," he said, "that you know what has happened to me, and what engaged me to undertake a long voyage?"

"You will soon know," replied the statue, "But before then, observe exactly what I am about to prescribe to you; the moments are dear, don't waste them. You see that domed hall twenty pace from here; it's necessary that you carry me into that place promptly, and there, I will tell you that it is necessary to do."

"Eh! How can I carry you," he said, "when it would be impossible for the combined strength of three men to do that?"

"You're mistaken," she replied. "Try and you'll see."

That design appeared to him to be ridiculous, but, having embraced the statue, he sensed that it was easy to detach it from the throne and pedestal, and, placing it on his shoulder, he found that it was no heavier than a person of mediocre height would have been.

On going into the hall he saw a huge vat of boiling water.

"Throw me into that vat," she said to him.

He dared not hesitate, and obeyed.

Gradually, the face of the beautiful person became animated and the colors of her body faded away. As he considered her attentively, the hall suddenly shook; a rain of fire fell upon the vat, and the statue cried: "I'm dying."

A single moment produced and dissipated that charm, and everything returned to its original condition. Boca saw the head of the statue inclined over the rim of the vat, the eyes closed like those of someone who has fainted. He took a step forward in order to approach, but he was stopped by the arrival of a man of extraordinary but imposing form.

The man lifted the head of the statue with one of his hands, and the other approached to her lips an open ivory box that he was holding. He received therein a little amber ball that emerged from her mouth, after which he closed the box and disappeared.

The statue awoke, as if from a profound sleep, and appeared to Boca to be the most beautiful person in the world.

"Go," she said to him. "Run to the marble palace. Touch the door with your little stick, go in, traverse the twelve chambers that precede the throne room, and when you have arrived there, tap the throne three times with your stick and wait for me; but above all, don't close any of the doors behind you. It will be beneficial to you, Boca, to have obeyed me. Go promptly, the instants are precious."

He had a great deal of difficulty as to the path he ought to take to return to the palace; the routes through the wood were confusing and it was necessary to go through the myrtle grove to regain the flower garden. Finally, allowing hazard to guide him, he took the first path that was presented to him, and after having walked for about seven or eight minutes he emerged from the wood and found himself in a beautiful avenue of orange trees, which led to an oval very similar to the one he had seen.

He realized that it was the grove parallel to that of myrtles, and without considering it further, he only perceived as he traversed it that instead of beehives, a large quantity of pineapples occupied the oval; the palisades were pomegranates and lemon trees and the grottoes were replaced by large sprays of fresh water, which seemed to rise up to the clouds and fall back into basins of different forms.

He followed a broad avenue that led straight to the palace. Immediately, curious to see the marvels that his little stick would produce, he struck the palace door, which opened instantly.

A slight fear gripped him, but, gathering his courage, he traversed the twelve chambers, taking great care to leave the doors open behind him, arrived in the last and saw a large throne of marble similar to that of which the statue was composed. He struck it three times with his stick, and, immediately changing its face, it was no longer anything but gold and precious stones.

A confused noise of horses, drums, trumpets and various musical instruments was heard, and a thousand cries of joy rising into the air caused the air to resound with the names of Abdelazis and Sedy Assan. Soon the interior of the palace was filled with people of both sexes; several guards placed themselves behind the throne and a host of courtiers, richly and elegantly clad, who had entered the room, formed a circle on both sides.

Three ladies of an extraordinary beauty advanced at a slow and majestic pace. The oldest was leaning on the shoulder of one of them, and holding the youngest by the hand. Boca believed that he recognized in the one on whom the lady was leaning the features of the woman that he had rescued in the forest, and in the one she was holding by the hand those of the beautiful statue, but, doubting what he saw, they believed that he was plunged in a profound slumber.

However, the three ladies approached him and bowed to him gracefully. The oldest addressed him. "Come, Boca," she said to him, "enjoy the happiness you have procured for this realm; thanks to you it is liberated from the tyranny in which its enemies have held it for a long time, and this beautiful princess has been saved by you from the most frightful torments."

Then, turning toward the youngest, she said: "Abdelazis, your liberator is taking everything he sees for an illusion; I'm touched by his trouble, let us render calm to his soul; you owe him the clarification of all this and the recompense for his labors. Let the action of your gratitude commence by not dissimulating any of the obligations you have to him; a heart born truly generous is glad to publish the benefits it has received; it is only permitted to ingrates to blush. I demand that you make him a sincere confession of the weaknesses that caused your misfortunes; ready to see them concluded, it will be less cruel for you to recall them. The generous Boca's heart is sufficiently interested for what is most dear to you; he will be better disposed to do what we expect of his courage. You have no need of me for that story, and you know that what remains for me to do will not permit any delay."

She embraced Abdelazis and left.

While the lady was speaking, everyone had been held in respect, maintaining a profound silence, but when she had finished, all those who were present threw themselves at the feet of the princess and testified to her the excess of their joy. She received them kindly, but soon escaped from their embraces. She extended her hand to Boca, and looked at the amiable person who accompanied her. "Come on, Zineby," she said, Let's take Boca to the Apartment of Astraea and have supper served to us there. We won't be interrupted, and I can begin to acquit a small part of what I owe him."

The princess having made a sign that she should not be followed, all three of them went into a broad gallery that led to the apartment in question. The place would have given Boca a great deal of admiration if he had been capable of having any for anything other than the beauty and graces of the princess.

It is true that Abdelazis could pass for a masterpiece of nature; she appeared to be in her seventeenth year at the most; her majestic bearing imprinted a respect that might have given birth to dread if her lively and touching eyes and a mild and gracious smile had not balanced that noble pride.

Zineby, four years older than the princess, endowed with a less regular beauty, assembled all the charms that a brilliant vivacity gives, mingled with delicacy and joviality.

They arrived at the door of the apartment, which was opened for them by two young girls clad in white and crowned with flowers. They traversed several rooms, simply but elegantly ornamented, where painted frescoes depicted the principal events that have immortalized the banks of the Lignon.[7]

---

[7] There are several rivers of this name in France but the one indicated here is the one that flows through Forez, on the banks of which Honoré d'Urfé's pastoral novel *L'Astrée* (1607-27; tr as *Astraea*) is set. The frescoes explain why the

The princess stopped in another, more spacious, the paintings of which represented a more modern history. Boca recognized other the portraits of the princess, Zineby, the lady he had just seen, and another woman that did not know, who was painted in some places in female attire, and in others dressed as a man. Her beauty attracted Boca's attention and the princess, fixing her eyes upon that amiable object said, while sighing: "Zineby, how much my happiness still lacks!"

Afterwards, having sat down at a table that had been prepared for her, she constrained Boca to take his place there. They were served by twelve young girls dressed like those who had opened the door of the apartment to them

During the meal, six young men elegantly dressed as shepherds made a concert of oboes and bagpipes, which repeated tender and rustic airs. As they left the table, the princess ordered everyone to withdraw, and, taking Boca by the hand, she made him sit down on a sofa, between her and Zineby.

"It is time," she said to him, "to talk to you about my misfortunes, and I am obeying with pleasure the command I have received to do so. More tranquil by virtue of the hope that has been reborn in my heart, I will tell you everything that I owe you, and why your help is still necessary to me.

---

apartment is called "the Apartment of Astraea," but not how such an apartment comes to be in a palace whose location appears to be very distant from France. Nor is it clear when the portraits in the apartment were painted, given the chronology of later developments in the story.

THE STORY OF PRINCESS ABDELAZIS

My father is the king of the Isle of Ebony. My grandparents, the king and queen, died within two months of one another and left my father their unique successor. Aged twelve, he was proclaimed king by unanimous consent, and the excellent qualities that were remarked in him gave hopes to his subjects that were fulfilled beyond their expectation. No governing prince has ever been seen with more wisdom, justice and generosity. At fourteen he married the princess of the Isle of Ivory. That choice pleased his subjects infinitely, and his estates hoped for great advantages therefrom. The princess had so much intelligence and grace that it was impossible to know her without loving her. The fay Beneficent protected her particularly; she is the lady you have just seen with us.

They did not desire fruits of their union for long; the queen became pregnant and when the term expired she gave birth fortunately. That was to me, to whom the name Abdelazis was given. I was born under fortunate auspices, which a sad destiny has since belied. The court and the people expressed their joy in magnificent fêtes, and the queen, following the custom of those who have a fay for a friend asked Beneficent to assemble several of her sisters to attend a superb banquet that she had prepared for them.

Perhaps you do not know, Boca, what happens in ceremonies of that sort; this is it. The invited fays, after having been regaled magnificently, ordinarily pass into the queen's apartment, to which the child in brought in the presence of the king and he grandees of the court.

One of them is elected protectress; it is ordinarily the friend of the queen who is chosen for that employment; the others each make a gift to the prince or princess, in accordance with their inclination or their power, and which is always limited from that moment on to the sole execution of those who have ordered it. The protectress does not make any gifts, in order to reserve a broader power and to balance and remedy the malignities of discontented or ill-intentioned fays.

Beneficent was appointed my protectress, and as she was sure of the good intention of the fays she had brought, she withdrew immediately in order to oppose those she suspected of coming to it with malevolent designs.

The oldest, to whom the honor reverted of speaking first, endowed me with wisdom; several others subsequently combined with that gift those of a tender, generous, beneficent heart; a solid and penetrating mind; a faithful memory and an accurate discernment. Three fays remained who had not yet spoken; one wanted me to have a particular facility for acquiring several talents; another gave me natural graces, and the last said, addressing the queen: "I am sorry to have been anticipated by my sisters; since very little remains for me to give the princess, I am ashamed to have nothing to offer her but beauty."

The queen did not find that gift as mediocre as she said, and would have been very sorry if it had been forgotten. She and the king thanked the fays with great demonstrations of gratitude.

As they were getting ready to withdraw, the fay protectress was seen to come in, followed by a tall, stiff woman with hollow cheeks, a livid complexion and sunken eyes; she was recognized as the fay Envious. As she approached they were all consternated; my protectress appeared to have had some quarrel with her, and I have found out since that Beneficent had argued for a long time to prevent her coming in, but, fearing to irritate her, she had been forced to yield.

Envious approached me. "Well, my sisters," she said, "continue, I beg you; I don't want to disturb your projects; on the contrary, will it not be permissible to add my benefits to yours? Tell me the gifts that have just been made to the princess, and I will try, if possible, to surpass them."

Those words reassured everyone, but no one hastened to satisfy her curiosity. However, it was necessary to confess everything to her, for she was beginning to be annoyed by the delay. All of the precious gifts that their amity had just accorded me were as many crimes for the fay Envious, but, dissimulating what was happening in her heart and applauding, with a forced smile, what the others had done, she said to them: "You have just formed an accomplished person; I shall think of making her happiness." After a moment's silence, she went on: "I want her to possess entirely the heart of Prince Kiribanou, my nephew, and that they both sense all the power of amour." After those words she withdrew.

The fays who saw nothing ominous in that present congratulated the king and queen, making them hope that those amours might form a great alliance, the fay's nephew being the son of a rich and powerful king of genii; but the protectress thought differently.

"I know Envious's nephew," she told them. "He must now be about ten years old. He is handsome and he has courage, but his mind, very advanced for his age, already full of artifices and suspicions, has earned him the nickname Prince Jealous. That passion is developing in him every day; what misfortune does it not announce for our dear princess! Envious is on bad terms with her brother, the king; she cannot see him without chagrin in possession of a rich and powerful kingdom. Often, in the war we have had against the genii, which is renewed from time to time, she has wanted, under various pretexts, to render him suspect to us and force us to turn our weapons against him alone. I fear that in wanting to unite these two hearts she has a desire to make both of them unhappy. I will employ all my art to help the princess, and I hope, my sisters, that you will aid me in that with your advice."

They all promised, and then they separated.

I was brought up with great care in the palace. My protectress often came to see me, and Envious also visited me sometimes, bring Prince Jealous with her.

One day, the fay protectress went into the queen's chamber and said to her: "I am sorry to have bad news to announce to you. I have discovered Envious's designs. She is going to ask you to allow Prince Jealous to live with the princess in the palace for a while; beware of refusing, she would like nothing better than that resistance, in order to have a pretext to abduct the princess; once she is in her power, you would lose her forever. Her goal, in making her marry the prince, is to exercise her tyranny over them and render them, by means of one another, the unhappiest of mortals.

"As she is very powerful I can see little remedy for those misfortunes; however, destiny has revealed to me that if the princess cannot see any other man than Prince Jealous until her fifteenth birthday, we shall be able to save her from the ill-fortune that is in preparation for her. In order to protect her from it, it is necessary to have a palace constructed in an isolated place where the princess will be brought up, that entry to it be forbidden to any man other than Prince Jealous, under penalty of death; that the guards have a league of avenues to forbid its approach; and finally, that all the women who are with her should never mention anyone but the prince, leaving her unaware that there are other men in the world.

"With those prudent precautions, I might perhaps be able to deflect the blows by which she is menaced, but if, by virtue of a power superior to mine, the malice of Envious prevails over me, at least the princess, only knowing Prince Jealous, having never made the comparison between him and another, will be able to regard his faults as the attributes of a sex different from her own. Her reason, her mildness, gratitude and habitude, might give birth in her heart to a sentiment that will help to overcome the antipathy that the opposition of their characters will naturally produce."

The queen approved that design, and, having communicated it to the king, work began on my retreat; the fay took charge of embellishing it and rendering it charming. That palace was built on the sea shore, ten leagues from the abode of the court. As soon as it was finished, I was taken there by the queen, my mother, and the fay protectress. A governess was chosen for me, maidservants, and several young girls to keep me company and to serve for my amusements; the women most celebrated for their science and their talents were employed for my education. I had scarcely reached my third year when I was imprisoned in that retreat. The queen left me there regretfully, promising to come to see me often, and relying on the care of the fay, whom she begged not to abandon me.

The king published throughout his kingdom the express prohibition to approach my dwelling, under penalty of death; in order to set an example he made the decision not to see me again until I reached my fifteenth birthday, and limited himself to the sole consolation of learning my news from the queen.

Six years went by without any remarkable event, and the queen came to spend a few days with me from time to time. Beneficent quit me as little as she could, and Envious and Prince Jealous rendered me fairly frequent visits. It was perceived from then on that the prince saw me with pleasure and only ever separated from me with chagrin. Envious took advantage of that disposition to ask for the favor that the prince remain in my retreat for a few months, which was granted on condition that he was only served there by my women, and that, in accordance with the decreed and published law, none of the men of his court would accompany him.

The prince was then fourteen and I was eight. In the first months we lived on good terms; he hastened to serve me, ceded everything without hesitation, and deprived himself of things given to him in order to sacrifice them to me, but, in his turn, he began to make demands on me proportionate to my age, which became very frequent and began to importune me. He had difficulty tolerating that the little girls who composed my little court received caresses from me. If they gave me fruits flowers if some trinket he was snatch them from their hands and opposed my accepting anything from anyone else.

Zineby, whom you see here, is the daughter of a lady of the palace, whom the queen liked very much. Although slightly older than me, she gained my amity more than any other, and the preference that I gave her over her companions appeared just to everyone but the prince. He conceived an aversion for her, which has made us both suffer since, and which contributed not a little thereafter to making me love her more.

She interrupted herself and turned her eyes to her companion tenderly. "Oh, my dear Zineby," she said to her, "how sweet it is for me to recall the moments we spent together! How many times your tender amity soothed my pains by making me see how sensible you were to them! Sometimes, your vivacity and gaiety charmed my anxiety; you did more, your advice was often a great help to me, and you have just given me a proof of attachment that has finished rendering us inseparable."

Zineby's only response was to kiss the hand of the princess, who continued speaking to Boca.

The prince followed me everywhere, and if sometimes, annoyed by his presence, I refused to admit him to our games, he made me bitter reproaches, troubled my diversions, quarreled violently with my friends, and threatened them with making them go away. My governesses represented to him in vain that more complaisance and mildness were necessary to please me; he responded with a proud scorn that since I was destined for him, it was necessary that I become accustomed to his fashion of acting.

In order to satisfy his jealousy, and find a means of not losing sight of me, he wanted to learn the same things that I was being taught and to receive the same lessons as me. He was soon chagrined by my progress and his unique occupation was no longer anything but tormenting me. Everyone in the palace hated him, and he became insupportable to me. I often complained to the queen and my protectress but they always excused him and engaged me to mildness.

We had already spent six months together when the war of the genii against the fays flared up again. The king, the father of Prince Jealous, demanded the return of his son from the fay, his sister. He wanted, by taking him with him into that war, to form him by example, and to second the ardor to which his impetuous character seemed to bear him. Envious could not refuse him what he desired. She came one day to tell the prince that he had to go away from me for some time. He appeared afflicted by that, but it was remarked that his dolor was more occupied with the displeasure of leaving me at liberty than the chagrin of losing me; his chagrin caused him to make abrupt adieux, and I received them with joy.

In spite of the politics that engaged my women to speak well of him to me and to bring me as much as they could to love him, I believed that I perceived that not one of them was sorry about his departure; however, when I sometimes complained about his humor to my governess, she represented to me that my duty demanded that I be sensible to the amity of the prince, that he would one day be my king, my master and my husband. That speech was repeated to me so many times by those who had authority over me, and his good qualities were exaggerated so strongly, that I persuaded myself that I had been wrong to hate him; his absence also aided his justification.

The life I led after his departure seemed to me to be so pleasant; everyone tried hard to please me and to procure me new diversions. I learned everything with enough facility, and I was left at liberty to be with

Zineby as much as I desired. We always had little secrets to tell one another; sometimes we meditated together on a new game for the following day; another time, Zineby, although instructed in the fashion in which she was supposed to talk to me about the prince, being more complaisant than the others, aided me in speaking ill of him.

One day when we were talking about him, I said, "Zineby, I wish that Prince Jealous resembled you; I wouldn't have so much difficulty in obeying him. But can't you tell me why all the girls that are here don't have a Prince Jealous who loves them, as I do? Because I'm a princess, why must I be more unfortunate than anyone else?"

Zineby replied to me, ingenuously: "It's to punish you, my princess, for being more beautiful than us, for having more intelligence and learning more rapidly. I've sometimes been angered about that, and it necessary that I love you very much to be able to pardon you."

That conversation was interrupted by some lessons in dance and music. My education was very singular; the unique objective of my retreat, as I've told you, was to leave me ignorant of the fact that there were other men than Prince Jealous in the world; people we obliged to conceal an infinite number of things from me that would have extracted me from my ignorance; the books that I was given to read, the pictures that were visible in the palace, the stories I was told—everything, in sum—was made expressly for the execution of that project. Among so many women it was difficult for no indiscretion to escape then, but my governess, who had a superior merit, watched over them with so much care that I didn't suspect anything of what was hidden from us; however, I often asked embarrassing questions.

One day, when the prince had been absent for eight months, I asked my governess where he was. She replied that he had gone with Envious to her realm.

"But what is that realm?" I asked her.

"It's a palace," she told me, "if which she is the princess, as you are here. Your protectress also has one, and as they're both fays, they have the power to go in and out of them as they please."

"But the queen, my mother, isn't a fay," I went on, interrupting her, "and she leaves her palace in order to me and see me. If I can't go where the fays live, can't I at least go with her?"

"It's necessary," she replied, "that you marry Prince Jealous before leaving here; then you'll be free to go where you desire, and he can take you to the queen's realm and even that of the fays, but he alone can give you that permission."

"I understand that," I said to her, sighing, "but you're not telling me why the queen has the liberty to come here. Did she have to marry a Prince Jealous, who permits her to do it?"

My governess, seeing that the conversation was going a little too far, fell back on the age of the queen, and told me that when I was as old as she was, I would be able to do the same things.

I wasn't satisfied by that reason and, giving in search of Zineby right away, I took her to the palace of pleasures; that was a small apartment built at the end of a long path in the park; it was filled with everything that could flatter and amuse our tender youth. Once a week I regaled my little court there; we were left at complete liberty there; one or two of my women accompanied me, but I was allowed to nominate those I desired to have. I had one key to it and my governess another; there was no study there, no remonstrations, no contrariety; I alone decided the games, everyone obeyed me, and I believed that I was only a princess in that place. I had demanded that no one ever mention Prince Jealous there, and people obliged me in that. That reason, more than any other, had engaged me to call it the palace of pleasures; everyone was accustomed to see Zineby and me going frequently to spend a couple of hours there.

That day, emerging from the conversation I had just had with my governess, we went into it, and after having locked the door behind us, I said: "Zineby, I have a chagrin. It's said that it's necessary to be the queen's age in order to get out of here, and only if Prince Jealous wants to permit it. Is he my master, then?"

"Console yourself, my princess," said Zineby. "The prince loves you; he'll grant you anything you desire."

"But I don't love him," I interjected, "and I'll never be able to bring myself to ask anything of him. No, no," I went on, with chagrin, "I'll refrain from having any obligation to him; I'd have to be grateful to him; I'd prefer him always to torment, me, in order to have reason to hate him. Oh, Zineby, how fortunate you are not to have been born a princess."

"But I have no lover," she replied, "and without the amity that I have for you, I feel that I might die if boredom. If we're separated, my princess, you'll always have something to occupy you; you'd soon choose one of my companions to relate your chagrins to, perhaps you'd love her more than me, because you'd need someone to listen to you. In the end, you'd forget the sad Zineby, who, having lost you, would no longer have anything to say or to think."

"Don't believe that, my dear friend," I said, embracing her. "I'll never love anyone but you."

Zineby said other things to me, the source of which I would have discerned at a more advanced age; they departed from an empty heart that her natural penchant bore to tenderness, and which, by virtue of gratitude and lacking any other object, took me for the one who had to fill it.

Our amity reached the point where we could not do without one another. We enjoyed two years of that pleasure without anyone raising any obstacle to it, but a truce that suspended the war between the genii and the fays brought Prince Jealous back to me. Envious did not fail to come with him as soon as he was free, and to present him to me as a young hero whose courage she praised to me with exaggeration.

I saw him again with chagrin, which I dissimulated as much as a person twelve years old can. The prince appeared to see with admiration the change he found in my person, and as if he had only commenced to love me on that day, he redoubled his jealous and tyrannical cares for me. He was no longer permitted to remain with me; the king, his father, had explained that to him before letting him leave; his politics made him approve of his amour, but he did not want his son wasting time with a child that was precious for his education, and he only permitted him to come to see me occasionally.

Envious favored her nephew by rendering rather frequent visits, and secretly nourishing a passion as unfortunate for the one who felt it as the one who was its object. Zineby soon became the object of his hatred; he begged Envious to separate us; we learned that, and our dolor was extreme.

I threw myself at the feet of the fay protectress and my mother, the queen, and, dissolving in tears, implored them to oppose that design. They promised me that, and obtained it with difficulty, but on the condition nevertheless that I only saw Zineby when the other girls were with me and we were never alone together. That order appeared to us to be mild by comparison with the misfortune by which we had been threatened, but how cruel its execution was!

Meanwhile, my aversion for the prince made as much progress as his amour; he remarked it with a furious chagrin, and did not neglect to make me feel its effects. Nevertheless, trying to borrow a character of mildness in order to persuade me, he depicted amour under a thousand different forms. Whatever penetration I had, however, I could not understand what my heart refused to feel; I responded to him in an embarrassed fashion: "Oh, Sire, why are your prayers not addressed to someone else? Am I the only person in the world that you can love?"

"Yes," the prince replied. "Only Abdelazis and Prince Jealous are made to live under the empire of amour and sense its sweetness." The prince was careful not to talk to me differently; he lent himself gladly to the ignorance of my education; it flattered his sentiments too well for him to want to dispel my illusion.

Gradually, I became accustomed to my slavery; I began to listen more patiently, and to try to give birth in my heart to a few sentiments of tenderness for him, but how little I knew of Amour! We can only flee him or obey him. My projects were futile; the only fruit of my efforts was that I acquired a little more power over my mind, but none over my heart. I forced myself to some complaisance, but not without an extreme violence.

My eyes often revealed the secret of my soul to my dear Zineby; I sometimes fixed them on hers with a languor penetrated with dolor.

I lived for two years in that sad situation; I was then fourteen, and the prince, whose passion augmented every day, engaged the fay Envious to ask my father for me in marriage. The truce was ready to end; he wanted to be united with me before the war obliged him to quit me.

That news was a thunderbolt for me; it was impossible for me to hide my dolor; I surrendered to it entirely. My protectress told me that if she could not break the marriage she could at least postpone its execution for a while, but I received scant consolation from that hope. As I dreaded Envious I had an idea of her power far superior to that of my protectress; however, it was balanced by the fashion in which she obtained that nothing would be concluded for six months. She hoped during that time to discover some means of prolonging it further, and as I was approaching my fifteenth year, and when that term expired I had nothing more to fear from Envious, she flattered herself that she might enable me to escape her malice.

She came to bring me that news with a joy that penetrated me with gratitude. The prince, chagrined and discontented, was in a worst humor; he heaped me incessantly with complaints and reproaches. Soon, however, he had a more sensible displeasure; the truce broke before the prescribed time and the war, which recommenced, obliged to him return to his father, the king, in order to command under his orders. Envious also had to go away.

I received that news one day when I was alone with the prince and my governess. It made an equally deep impression on us, although the reasons for that were different; my joy could only be compared with the prince's dolor; I had difficulty containing it, but he, being more reckless, yielded to the emotions that agitated him.

"Oh, cruel woman," he said to me, "You're triumphant at my unhappy fate! The malign joy you feel cannot escape the penetration of a lover's hate. Let that joy burst forth, then, in order that my hatred might increase; may it equal yours and finally force me to punish you."

"If I do not have for you, Sire," I replied, "all the amour that you desire, who ought you to blame for that? I have done what I can to give birth to it in my heart; perhaps I would have succeeded, if it were not for your unjust persecutions."

That reproach inflamed his anger, and he launched a gaze at me full of fury. "I have suffered too much," he said, "from an ingrate who still dares to outrage me. Since my amour and my cares have been unable to touch her, let her at least fear me. Tremble, unfortunate princess; I shall soon return victorious over our enemies; if you do not grant me your heart and your hand then, tremble; death is less cruel than the fate I am preparing for you."

He left as soon as he had pronounced that terrible words, and my governess, seized by fear like me, criticized me for having irritated him by means of a reproach that was, indeed, just, but whose consequences I ought to have foreseen.

His absence dissipated my dread, and my first concern was to ask my protectress for the return of Zineby. She granted me that, and we had the liberty to see one another as much as we desired. I had so many things to tell my friend that I would have liked to add to the hours of the day those of the night. In order to be freer, the two of us went on our own every day to the palace of pleasures to spent a few hours before supper.

A short time after the departure of the prince, Beneficent came to bid me adieu. Your enemies are occupied, Princess," she said to me. "I have nothing to fear from them in leaving you here. Your interests summon me elsewhere; it's necessary that I find more arms to oppose the malign Envious; I have to profit from this time to thwart her designs. Adieu, my dear Abdelazis; I hope to free you from the calamitous destiny that threatens you, and if I only have the power of Envious to combat, everything will succeed in accordance with my desires."

I did not understand the fay's final words, and, relying on her tenderness, I abandoned myself to the hope that she gave me.

Three days after her departure, I gave a fête in the palace of pleasures. It was magnificent; we spent all day there. The next day, I returned there alone with Zineby, and as the heat of the day was great I proposed to her that we go for a walk toward the sea, hoping to find a cool breeze there. Gradually, we covered a considerable distance, and we approached the shore. The waves, whitened by foam, were in a rather violent agitation, which caused us to stop to consider the spectacle.

What was our astonishment, however, when we saw a young and beautiful person lying on the sand! She seemed to be profoundly asleep. Her attire differed from ours; a white robe embroidered with gold and enriched by pearls and specious stones of different colors descended to her feet; although it was soaked with water, its splendor and richness attracted Zineby's admiration.

Only occupied with the charms of her person, however, I said: "What is amusing you? Look at those features, that mild expression, the graces spread over that amiable face! That hair, in spite of the dampness of the waves, has lost nothing of its beauty. No, Zineby, I have never seen anything similar. Let's find out who this young woman is. Let's wake her up; I'm dying of impatience to learn what brought her to this place."

I bent down and, taking the hand of the stranger, I woke her up.

Her first gaze fell upon me, and saw a fire shining there that completed making her seem charming to me. The sight of me seemed to surprise her, and she got up precipitately.

"O gods," she cried, "all the beauties of the earth combined are offered to my gaze." Immediately throwing herself at my feet, she continued: "I believed that my death was about to satisfy the wrath of the gods, but whatever my destiny might be henceforth, I ought not to complain of it, since they have permitted me to adore in you their most perfect work."

That praise appeared to me to be excessive, but as I felt inclined to love the person who had given it to me, I pardoned her easily.

"Why do you want to die?" I said to her, holding out my hand to lift her up. "No, my dear girl, you shall live; I want to take care of your days."

Zineby seconded the caresses I made her; she received them with a kind of confusion and much grace.

The need she had of changing clothes made us take the path to the palace of pleasures. I interrogated her as to her birth and asked her what fay had brought her to that place.

She seemed reluctant to reply, and asked me to wait until she had taken a little repose before satisfying me. Having pressed her at least to tell me her name, she said, after a moment's silence: "My name is Zobeide; but you, charming person, will you not tell me who you are and what realm I am in?"

"You're in my realm," I told her, "and my name is Abdelazis."

At those words she seemed to fall into a profound reverie.

However, we arrived at the palace, and, Zineby having brought the apparel of one of my women, we both wanted to help Zobeide put it on, but out of respect for my rank she did not want to allow that.

We left her at liberty, and Zineby and I retired to the next room. "My dear friend," I said to her, "I'm in a strange anxiety. What are we going to do with Zobeide?"

"We'll take her to the palace," she replied, "and I have no doubt that all my companions will be pleased to see her augment your court; she will be dear to them, since she has been able to please their princess."

"No, no, you're mistaken, Zineby, she would cause jealousy, and I would lose her. How do I know whether my governess would permit her to stay with us? I even dread that someone might surprise us. If you love me, help me to hide her, at least for a few days. But how? The sun is about to set; we have to go. Tell me, then, what do you want me to do? You can't think of anything? Oh, Zineby, you don't have as much intelligence as usual today."

"But, my princess," she said, "you haven't given me time to think."

"That," I replied, "is because your tender amity has always anticipated my wishes. Forgive my agitation; I don't know what to do."

"This is what I think," she said. "Let's leave Zobeide here; she'll find some of the things she needs here, and I'll take charge of the rest. You come here every day; you'll see her, and to avenge myself for the quar-

146

rel you've just had with me, I'll share that pleasure with you."

I approved her idea, and after embracing tenderly, we went to find Zobeide.

We told her that important reasons forced us to leave her in that solitude, that she wouldn't lack anything, and that we would tell her more the next day.

"Oh," said Zobeide sighing, "I shall lack everything, since I'm losing you; you're going to quit me."

"It's necessary, my dear girl," I replied, "but it won't be for long. I implore you, however, not to go out of this palace unless we permit you to." We embraced her, and returned to the palace later than usual; reproaches were made to me, but my caresses had soon appeased the most severe.

Zineby perceived the anxiety that was agitating me. She sometimes smiled at me, but I only responded with a sigh.

She escaped from us after suffer, and I didn't see her for two hours. I saw her come back in thereafter, and she approached me.

"I've just rendered you a service," she whispered."

I squeezed her hands without replying, and, les anxious, I tried to resume my ordinary gaiety.

The next day, the hour when I had the custom of going to the palace of pleasures seemed to come with a slowness that made me despair. It arrived; Zineby and I left. Zobeide saw me again with a joy that augmented mine. I found her more beautiful than the previous day, but the vivacity of her eyes was combined with a languor that afflicted me; I feared that it might be caused by the ennui of finding herself alone in the palace.

I did what I could to engage her to stay for a few more days in that solitude, and, having told her that the dread of dooming her made me take those precautions, that as I depended on the queen, my mother, two fays and Prince Jealous, who could not suffer that I had friends, I had reason to believe that I would not be permitted to keep her with me.

Those words troubled her, and, fixing her eyes on mine she said: "Oh, Abdelazis, you have a lover, then? A lover favored by fays—and doubtless loved by you," she added, with a sigh.

"I wish to heaven," I replied, "that I had amour for him; I would not have so much to lament. But Zobeide, let us only talk about you. I leave it to Zineby to tell you the secret of my heart; tell me who you are, and what brought you to this place."

"I am," she replied, "an unfortunate persecuted by relatives. Not long ago, I lost those from whom I obtained life; they possessed considerable wealth in a realm distant from yours. They confided my youth to people to whom I ought to have been dear, but who, not content with having usurped the wealth that belonged to me, conceived the design to make sure of it by means of my death. They attempted my life several times, and constrained me to flee my homeland in order to escape their cruelty.

"A small number of people attached to me took charge of conducting me to a place where I would have nothing to fear for my days. They put me on a ship, and their amity caused them to share with me the dangers of the sea; but the gods, reserving for me the good fortune of falling into your hands, excited a furious tempest yesterday, by which our ship, after having been agitated by the wind for some time, was eventually broken by lightning and dispersed in a thousand fragments.

"I shall not depict for you the horror that accident cast among us. It was so prompt that we did not have time to regret life. A residuum of hope made me seize a plank that, pushed by the winds, carried me as far as the shore.

"It was there, my beautiful princess, exhausted by fatigue, that I yielded to slumber, or rather to my weakness. I saw you, and, forgetting all my misfortunes, I felt joy born in my heart, hope, and…."

She lowered her eyes without finishing; but Zineby, seeing that I was allowing a few tears to escape, said: "What's the matter, my princess? You're weeping?"

"You ought to be ashamed of not doing likewise," I told her. "Zobeide has seen herself ready to lose her life, and you're not weeping? What! That sad story hasn't moved you?"

"I enjoy the pleasure of seeing her delivered from it," she replied, "and her present good fortune effaces in me the impressions of her past troubles."

Zobeide was about to speak, but we heard a noise in the next room; I was seized by dread and promptly shut her in a cabinet, the key of which I took. It was my governess and some of my women. They were looking for me in order to inform me that the queen would be arriving in three days, and that she was to stay with me until the return of the fay Beneficent.

I received that news with a disturbance that nearly doomed me, but Zineby, who perceived it, diverted their suspicions by telling them the story of a pretended conversation that we had just had on the subject of Prince Jealous. We were obliged to retire with everyone else.

The next day we returned to see Zobeide, and were surprised to find the door of the palace open. I went in precipitately, and, not seeing her, I called to her several times, in vain.

"She isn't here!" I cried. "We've been discovered. Oh, I'm doomed!"

"What, my dear princess?" Zineby said to me. "Abdelazis? Is it you talking? What an excess of dolor! Doubtless Zobeide, seeking to dissipate her ennui, must have wanted to take a walk while awaiting the hour for us to arrive; and as your impatience has brought you here early, we'll see her return imminently."

Those words calmed me down, but, seeing me plunged in a profound sadness, she continued "Ah! If Zineby were lost to you, would you be so afflicted. No, a stranger has overtaken me in three days, alas. I've always thought so; you're too lovable not to have my entire heart, but I'm not enough to prevent you from dividing yours."

That reproach suspended my initial dolor momentarily, and I took Zineby's hand. "How cruel you are," I said to her, "to add to my pain an error that I don't want to make. No, I wouldn't pardon myself for loving Zobeide like you; also, it isn't like you that I love her; our amity, formed by long habitude, has augmented insensibly; the charms of your intelligence, your mildness, your kindness, the marks of your tenderness, have attached me to you by gentle and tranquil bonds. But what I feel for Zobeide is mingled with a trouble and an agitation that banishes peace from my heart; I even believe that I hate the day that enabled me see her for the first time. Would you want me, Zineby, to love you like that? Deadly as the sight of Zobeide is for me, however, I sense that if I lose her, there are no more pleasures for me. Do not let your generous amity abandon me; on the contrary, help me to search for her everywhere; and if you return her to me, count on my loving you as much as you wish, and you will not have to complain of me any longer."

At those words, Zineby stood up. "I think," she said, "that it's appropriate for you to remain here while I go into the park to search for Zobeide. If your women have seen her, I believe it to be prudent that you don't appear to have taken so much interest in her."

I yielded to that discourse and let her leave, She had scarcely gone than I found that it was taking her too long to come back.

Zineby, however, ran from path to path, giving every care to her search. Having seen two of my women coming out of an arbor that terminated a long pathway she slipped behind a palisade and let them pass. When she had lost sight of them she went into the arbor and was very surprised to find Zobeide there, sitting on a bank, plunged in a profound reverie.

"Oh, Zobeide," she said to her, "why are you here? What have those women said to you who have just left here?"

"They didn't see me," Zobeide replied. "I was hidden behind that palisade. But where is the princess?" she added, precipitately.

Zineby having told her about the dread and anxiety in which she had left me in the palace of pleasures, I saw them both return with a joy that cannot be expressed. I reproached Zobeide for the fears she had caused me, and had the pleasure of seeing her so touched by it that I could not hold it against her that she had given birth to it. I implored her not to expose me to such troubles again.

She asked me the name of my protectress, and when she learned that it was Beneficent she appeared transported by joy. She told us that the fay had been a friend of her mother, and that she hoped for her protection; however, she begged us not to anticipate her and to leave her the care of making herself known.

We promised her that, and I flattered myself that one day, I would be able to see her with the same liberty and as often as Zineby.

A few days later my mother arrived; I loved her tenderly, but I could not see without an extreme trouble the obstacle that she raised by her presence to the pleasure I experienced in spending a few hours every day with my dear Zobeide. It was necessary for me to resolve to deprive myself of that, and I soon became jealous of the liberty that Zineby had to see her.

I fell into a depression that made everyone anxious. The queen often asked me the reason for it, but I was obstinate in hiding it from her and feigned illness one day in order to have the liberty to speak at length with Zineby. I shut myself in my room and said that I wanted to rest.

When we were alone, I said to her, in a rather chilly fashion: "Well, Zineby, you see Zobeide every day, then; do you believe now that you're more fortunate than me and that the fate of a princess is as fine as you've sometimes imagined? See the constraint I'm in; for four days I haven't been able to escape for a moment, but you have liberty."

"You wouldn't reproach me, Princess," Zineby said to me, "if I hadn't used it to visit our new friend, and as I've always been with you, she has all the honor of being regretted."

"That honor scarcely touches you," I replied, "and the pleasure of seeing you compensates her adequately for my absence."

"Oh! For the first time I find you unjust!" she replied, hotly. "What! You don't think that my tender amity ought to be alarmed by that which you have for another? You don't see that my concern for her has no other object than the desire to please you? And without being touched by the sadness that Zobeide feels because of a cruel absence, you accuse us both of forgetting you?"

"Alas, dear Zineby," I said, "pardon the disturbance of my heart. I don't know at present whether I love or hate Zobeide; help me to figure out what my sentiments are, or, rather, confirm for me the resolution that I'm making at this moment not to see her again. Yes, she's fatal to my repose; I ceased to enjoy any the moment she was offered to my sight; I don't know the trouble and agitation that I'm feeling, and to confess everything—would you believe it? I can't tell you without blushing—the presence of the queen importunes me, her cares embarrass me, and I no longer find myself as affectionate toward her as I have been previously. What completes my confusion, and proves my injustice to me, Zineby, is that I feel that it wouldn't take much for me to love Zobeide as much as you; but I can assure you, at the same time, that you've never been dearer to me.

"Yes," I continued, embracing her and letting the tears flow that I had had so much difficulty holding back, "I love you as much as I am capable of doing, and you know my heart; I even sense that I owe you that tenderness, but I don't know what draws me toward Zobeide. Forgive, dear friend, an involuntary insult; I want to punish myself for it. Since that stranger has caused me to fail in the duties I owe to blood and amity, let's not see her any longer. Reveal everything to my governess; I charge you with that care. Tell her what has occurred, and, whatever might happen, I shall submit to anything rather than remain in the state I'm in."

"But if you're accorded what you're asking," Zineby said, "and Zobeide is expelled from the palace, remember that you will never see her again."

"Oh, how cruel you are," I replied. "Why not hope, on the contrary, that on finding her so lovable, they will make it a pleasure to keep her here? Perhaps they'll approve of my loving her, and I won't have need any longer of the secrecy and mystery for which I reproach myself."

The queen came in at that moment and interrupted us. I wasn't possible for me to revoke the order that I had given Zineby, of which I was beginning to repent, and when I saw her leave my room I shivered at what she was about to do. My anxious and embarrassed manner made the queen believe that I was paying too much attention to my illness, and, wanting to distract me, she summoned women who played several musical instruments perfectly. She ordered them to form a concert, hoping that that might alleviate the state that I was in. That sort of distraction suited me better than any other; it exempted me from talking and excused my reverie.

Zineby had retired alone after having quit me, and, passing over in her mind all the ideas to which our recent conversation had given birth, her sentiments for me, those that I had for her, and the comparison she made of the new movements of my heart with those she had always known, her intelligence and the penetration she had made her suspect that an absolute power was determining my heart, but the ignorance of her education, which had been similar to mine, prevented her from divining its author. Seeking to enlighten herself, instead of going to see my governess, as I dreaded, she took the path to the palace of pleasures.

She perceived Zobeide, who was coming toward her precipitately. "The suffering is too great," she said to her, as she approached. "It's necessary that I see the princess, or I'll die."

"You won't die," said Zineby, "and you'll return with me this instant to a place that you've been forbidden to quit, and where Abdelazis wants you to stay."

She had difficulty consenting to that, and it was only after having assured her that she would incur my disgrace if she didn't obey.

When they were secure, Zineby, who had her designs, gave birth in her heart, by turns, to dread, hope and jealousy, and, remarking her fear her transports and her hatred for Prince Jealous, she was confirmed in her suspicions. However, Zobeide was obstinate in wanting to see me, and assured her that her life was at stake. Zineby promised to find a means, and begged her to wait until the next day.

I didn't know what had happened, and the next day, seeing her come into my room laughing and cheerful. I said to her: "You take very little part in the ennui that is tormenting me; and if you've carried out the order that I gave you yesterday, it's announcing my misfortune with a very serene countenance."

"I refrained carefully from obeying you," said Zineby, "and I saw clearly that you were deceiving yourself in thinking that you wanted me to do as you said. I know you better, my princess, and in consequence, I was able to refuse you and anticipate you. For example, you wanted to hide from me the extreme desire that you had to see Zobeide, and I intend that you shall, today."

"Oh, you're rendering me life," I said, embracing her, "but how will you do it?"

"Allow yourself to be guided," she said. "Propose to the queen this evening spending a few hours in the park, and let me take care of the rest."

I did as she asked. The excursion was agreed. Everyone followed the queen there. The weather was admirable, delightfully cool, and the stars were so bright that one could see well enough to direct oneself without the help of the moon. We stayed there for a long time and, seeing that no one had anything to say to me, I told Zineby, in a piqued fashion, loud enough for everyone to hear me that I wanted to retire and be left alone. Zineby started to laugh, without replying, and I couldn't express how I felt about her at that moment.

I arrived in my room with the design of shutting myself in.

As she was returning to the palace, the queen was told that a woman wanted to speak to her on the part of the fay protectress; she went to her apartment in order to talk to her, and I forbade anyone whatsoever to enter mine before bed-time. Then my tears flowed in abundance, and I abandoned myself to my chagrin and my dolor.

Soon, however, a small cabinet opened and I saw Zineby emerge with Zobeide. She threw herself at my knees with a transport that troubled me; for a few moments we did not say anything, and then, both breaking the silence at the same time, our confused speech, our joy and our tears informed Zineby fully. It was, however, necessary for us to separate; how cruel that moment was!

Zineby took Zobeide back to the palace of pleasures.

They had scarcely gone out when the queen came into my room; she had come to tell me that Beneficent would arrive the following day. I feared and desired the fay's return. I assured the queen that the news gave me an extreme pleasure. Zobeide was informed of it, and, making her resolution, she wrote a letter that she handed to Zineby to give to the fay, without telling her what it contained. She only asked her to make sure that Beneficent was alone when she gave it to her.

I was informed of those circumstances by Zineby and I had a great desire to read that letter and prevent her from delivering it, but the fear of annoying Zobeide retained me.

On her return, the fay covered me with caresses, and after saying several things, asked me how I had spent the time. That question embarrassed me so much that, having lowered my eyes, it was impossible for me to find a word to reply to her. For the first time, she saw my face covered with a blush that made her understand that something strange as happening in my heart. She did what she could to reassure me, and, seeing that I was becoming more and more embarrassed in trying to talk to her, out of pity for me she summoned Zineby, in order to discover the reason for my trouble. It increased violently when I saw the fatal moment approaching when the fay would discover my secret; unable to sustain her presence I withdrew, and left her alone with Zineby.

It is not possible for me to depict for you the emotions that agitated me then; of all pains, uncertainty is the most cruel. I found Zineby again when she emerged from the fay's apartment and ran to her.

"Well," I said, "did you give her the letter? Has the fay read it? What did she say? Is Zobeide going to be taken away from me?"

"The letter has been read," she replied, "but I don't know what Beneficent thinks; she didn't say anything to me."

"Oh, Zineby," I said, "If I'd been there, I would have divined it."

"You'll know very shortly," she said, "for she charged me with telling me that she wants to talk to you."

I shivered at that discourse, and Zineby had difficulty determining me to go to see the fay.

She received me with open arms, and as soon as she saw me she said: "Come, Abdelazis, to receive a pardon that you have not yet asked of me. I know the mystery that you have made in my regard, but I'm not as offended by it as your friend, so, only expect tender reproaches from me. Why did you fear that I would oppose your desires? You know how much I love you, so don't hide from me anything you have in your heart. Have I prevented you from seeing and loving Zineby? Did you believe that I would be more severe for Zobeide?"

Those words reassured me and I threw myself at her feet. "Oh, Madame," I said, "How your kindness augments the reproaches I have made myself!"

"I see nothing," she went on, "that ought to trouble you, except for the secret that you have kept from me, which I no longer want to remember. The rest is quite simple. I can only approve your pity for an amiable individual whom hazard enabled you to encounter. It is a grandeur of soul, Abdelazis, to help the unfortunate. But, my dear girl, there is something more important that ought to occupy you. The war is over; we have vanquished the rebel genii, and Prince Jealous will soon demand your hand and conclude your marriage; all my art cannot protect you from that. You're shivering! What! The virtue that we have cultivated in you with so much care cannot overcome your aversion? The prince adores you; are you not at least susceptible to gratitude?"

"Oh, Madame," I cried, "my heart is penetrated by it for anyone other than him; but ought I to have for him sentiments that resemble hatred more than amour? I believed that I could accustom myself to that fashion of being loved, but Madame, your kindness, Zineby's tenderness—in sum, everything I experience of amity—appears to me preferable to the prince's tyrannical passion, and leaves no place for him in my heart. I even sense that it might cost me my life if I cannot avoid being his forever."

"Well," said the fay, "there is still one means of saving you from that marriage. Zobeide has hidden her birth from you, but I know it. She was born a princess like you; let her marry Prince Jealous; perhaps we will be able to make him consent to a change in her favor. She's beautiful, and will soon be mistress of a great realm. What do you think, Abdelazis?"

"What, Madame!" I replied. "You could deliver her to the most frightful fate?"

"But perhaps Zobeide might not think like you," she said, "and would be flattered by the conquest of the prince."

"No, no," I replied, precipitately. "She isn't made to love him. I can even assure you that she hates him as much as I do. But that's not all; the prince would soon refuse me the pleasure of seeing her; he wouldn't be able to tolerate the amity there is between us, and I can't be separated from her."

"You can't be separated from her, Abdelazis! What, then, are her charms so powerful that they have given birth to such a strong amity in such a short time?"

"You know her," I replied. "Can you ask me that?"

"I know that she is beautiful," the fay said, "but what if the person that seems to you to be charming were metamorphosed by my art into a hideous form, what sentiment would you have for her then?"

"Everything that I feel at present," I replied. "Her misfortune would only render her dearer to me; I would rediscover her heart, her mind and her tenderness; she would love me more, because I would perhaps be the only friend that remained to her. But Madame, whatever your power might be, Zobeide can never cease to be lovable."

"That's enough," said Beneficent. "I'll take care of Zobeide. But Princess, it's no longer permitted for you to see her without my order. Have the keys to the palace of pleasures brought to me immediately; I want to forbid anyone to approach it, and I don't want anyone to know the reason. Refrain carefully, Abdelazis, and you, Zineby, from revealing a secret that it is important to hide. Zobeide's life and yours, Princess, would be in a danger from which it might not be possible for me to extract you. That's sufficient, I think, to engage you to obey me."

Immediately, the fay quit me in order to go to Zobeide.

I did not know how that conversation went; my anxiety was extreme. I accused Beneficent of being even crueler than the fay Envious. Zineby, you saw my affliction and you know how I suffered during a week of absence. I did not know whether Zobeide was still in the palace of pleasures; the fay assured me of it, but I had too much dread to believe her.

Finally, my tears and sighs softened her, but great gods, on what condition was I permitted to see her again! It was necessary for me to promise to marry Prince Jealous. I hesitated for a long time, but in the end, the attraction of a present joy prevailed over the idea of a frightful future; we departed with Zineby

As I got closer, the surge of joy that had seized me diminished and gave way to the dread of being deceived in my hope. *Alas*, I said to myself, *perhaps the fay has banished Zobeide from this place forever, and she is only taking me to this sad palace in order to conceal my extreme dolor from everyone; she does not want anyone to know its cause, and it's in this solitude that I am going to learn my misfortune. Oh, palace of pleasures, you will no longer be anything to me but a place of horror!*

We arrived; as we went in I looked in all directions, and, not seeing Zobeide, I threw myself on to a sofa and abandoned myself to my dolor. The fay spoke. "Cease to afflict yourself," she said. "You will soon see Zobeide, but Princess, lend me all your attention; I am going to reveal an important secret to you."

Then she unveiled to me the mystery of my education, and told me that, not being able to prevent me belonging to Prince Jealous, she had hoped that ignorance, habitude and gratitude would achieve in me what amour could not. Then she represented to me what duty demanded of me.

"I flatter myself," she went on, "that it will be stronger than my cares; you have received many gifts from us, Abdelazis; will the most precious of all, virtue, be useless to you?"

"No, Madame," I replied, "And since it is necessary to yield to my destiny, I expect powerful assistance from that virtue. I know what I owe to the cares of your amity; it is time to render myself worthy of it."

"Pardon, my dear princess," said Beneficent, "a prison that has saved you from great dangers. Alas, our tender youth would have exposed you at court to the deadly poison of amour; perhaps you would have blushed at it too late, and sentiments innocent in appearance would have deceived you and perhaps made dangerous progress involuntarily. A noble pride might have brought you back to your duty in vain, and it would have cost you dear to combat and vanquish a flattering and seductive penchant; perhaps you would now be in the utmost depths of misfortune. Amour, Abdelazis, takes all kinds of forms, but virtue is able to unmask it."

She stood up then, and told us to wait for her. I fell into a reverie, which gave Zineby the opportunity to make many reflections on what we had just learned.

We saw the fay return with Zobeide, but what was my surprise on seeing her dressed like Prince Jealous! Beneficent, in presenting me to her, said: "Princess, recover from your error; it is no longer Zobeide that you see; it is Prince Sedy Assan whom fortune enabled you to encounter on the shore, to whom I shall soon return a throne that his enemies have stolen from him,"

I remained in the grip of a disturbance and a shame that robbed me of the usage of speech; in a moment, everything I had just learned, being retraced in my mind, caused me to condemn what was happening in my heart. Sedy Assan remained at my feet, almost as confused as I was. By means of her gaze, Zineby was showing us both her tenderness, and the fay, examining us, interpreted our silence.

Finally, the prince spoke. "Oh, Madame," he said to me, "how do you see Sedy Assan? Can I flatter myself that you will remember Zobeide?"

"Let us forget Zobeide," I said to him, blushing. "Why, Prince, have you deceived me?"

Then I begged the fay to permit me to withdraw momentarily with Zineby, unable to sustain in their presence the various emotions by which I was agitated.

When we were alone, I said: "My dear Zineby, what have I just learned? Alas, why was I not left in my ignorance? It would always have been permitted to me to love Zobeide, but Prince Sedy Assan....oh, how difficult it is for me to separate them! I tremble for her days, I have no hope, and I love her, I love her.... No, no, I don't believe it, Zineby, I am making a monster of the innocent amity to which you have given birth; but will it be forbidden for me to love in the prince everything that I see in him that is great, noble and virtuous? I don't feel capable of that injustice, and I reproach myself for it. Yes, let us allow my heart to render the homage that is due to him; do you not love him as I do, do you think that it is a crime?"

"I loved him as you did," she said to me, embracing me. "Oh, Princess, what a difference! It's no longer time, my dear Abdelazis, to have a feeble complaisance for you; I reproach what has brought me until now to serve an amour that will cost you too much pain. I engaged myself in that by ignorance, but a few days ago, seeking to discern your sentiments and seeing at the vivacity of your progress was about to cause your misfortune, I resolved, out of pity, to wait for more powerful aid in order to combat them. Have no more doubt about it, Abdelazis, you love Sedy Assan as you ought to have loved Prince Jealous. Beneficent told you, a moment ago, that amour takes all forms in order to deceive us; she depicted for you then the present state of your heart, and opposed to its sentiments those that virtue ought to inspire in you. I feel for you; I sense your dolors, I excuse your weakness, but I love you too much to aid you in your error."

"Yes, my dear friend," I replied. "You've opened my eyes. and you'll see whether I'm worthy of the amity that you have for me. Let's return to the fay."

I got up instantly. I found the prince on his knees, dolor painted on his face. It would not have taken much t that moment for me to forget my resolutions. However, addressing Beneficent, I said: "Madame, if you love me, take the prince away from here as soon as possible. I do not want to see him again. But Madame, I ask you at the same time, for a favor; whether I am forced to marry Prince Jealous, or whether I avoid that misfortune, do not suffer that I ever quit this solitude. I am resolved to spend the rest of my days here. Renew the severe orders that forbid anyone to approach it; let my women and the young girls who have been brought up with me return to the court; a few slaves will be enough to serve me."

Then I turned to Zineby. "I shall not order your fate," I said. "Whatever decision you make, I will never cease loving you."

Zineby, pressing my hands tenderly in hers, moistened them with tears, was scarcely able to pronounce the words: "I shall only quit you in the tomb."

My only response was to hug her in my arms.

The prince threw himself at Beneficent's feet, and that spectacle made her mingle her tears with those we were all shedding. Then she spoke. "My daughter," she said to me, "I cannot condemn a penchant that only virtue can overcome, but it is necessary to obey destiny and show what duty can do. The prince must go; a ship is waiting for him on the shore, and I will take him to it. Stay here. If you believe me, spare yourself adieux in the course of which you might show weakness."

"Oh, Madame," I cried, "why do you mistrust me, since I am demanding that he go away myself? I must flee Sedy Assan, but may I not render Zobeide one last duty of amity?"

We took the road to the sea; I believed that I saw despair in Sedy Assan's eyes, but I accused him secretly of not being sufficiently opposed to our separation. I did not know then the reasons that engaged him to silence.

The fatal moment arrived. We were close to the ship; he was about to leave when a mortal chill gripped me; my strength abandoned me; pallor covered my fact, and I fainted.

"Is that enough, Madame?" cried Sedy Assan. "Is it necessary for her to die to touch you? Oh, my princess, all the powers of the world combined can never separate us; I would perish a thousand times rather than abandon you."

"That's it, I give in, Prince," the fay interrupted. Then she commanded genii to carry me on to the ship. She had Zineby board the vessel, and when she had embarked with the prince it departed instantly, and we covered an immense distance in a moment.

The fay extracted me from my faint, and I saw the prince at my feet. "What!" I said to him, turning my eyes away in order not to see him. "Dolor has not deprived me of life? Do you think I can survive the shame of my weakness?"

"Live, live, my princess!" he cried. "Live for Sedy Assan; all my wishes are fulfilled. It is no longer forbidden to you to show your sentiments. If they are favorable to me, don't blush, charming Abdelazis; I aspire to the happiness of being your husband."

What I heard, and the new objects that were presented to my eyes, all made me believe that it was only a dream, but the fay soon undeceived me, and told me that, wanting to test whether I veritably felt amour, she had agitated all the springs of my soul; that she had no more doubt that Envious's prediction, and the one she had read in destinies, would be accomplished.

Hazard had led Prince Sedy Assan, fleeing a cruel usurper, to be shipwrecked close to the place where I was; fearing that he had fallen into in an enemy country allied with his tyrant, he had been glad to see that his garments allowed him to be mistaken for a girl; he had seized the opportunity to hide and had lent himself to our error. Subsequently, amour and the fear of being removed from it had confirmed it. Two days after his arrival, he had overheard the conversation of two women in the arbor where Zineby had found him; without being seen, he had learned from their discourse the secret of my education and the peril of death that threatened him if he were discovered. Finally, finding a friend in my protectress, he had confessed everything he felt for me in his letter.

Since then, she had done everything possible to save me from the misfortune into which she feared that passion would draw me. She had forbidden the prince to make his own manifest, but, seeing that it was impossible for us to overcome it, she had finally consented to my happiness.

I assured her of my gratitude, and did not dissimulate my joy; the prince could not contain his own, and

Zineby reminded me that all that had not escaped her penetration.

The fay interrupted us to tell us that we were about to arrive in the prince's estates. Addressing Sedy Assan, she said: "Perhaps you believe that I am going to engage you in a cruel war, of which you hope for a successful outcome thanks to my help. Prince, that is not the way that Beneficent serves those she loves. The usurper of the Isle of Marble, in snatching your forefathers' scepter from you, attracted my hatred; the same motive that bears me to help the unfortunate also makes me punish the guilty. The week that appeared to the two of you to be so cruel was employed in serving my vengeance and seeking a means to protect you from the evil fate that menaces you. Sedy Assan, you will see your subjects returned to your obedience. The tyrant is dead and your people are waiting for you impatiently. The slave genii who are submissive to my orders have carried out those I have given to them. You only have to fear Envious and Prince Jealous; their rage will soon burst forth; they are powerful, but the present that I am going to make you might be able to save you from their fury.

Then she gave the prince the little wand that you have, Boca, which has operated so many marvels. "It's necessary," she continued, "that you conserve it careful-ly. Always carry it on your person, and I guarantee that all their efforts will be vain; but if it escapes you, your doom is certain.

"As for you, Abdelazis, listen carefully to what I am going to tell you. Here is an ivory box, in which all the art of enchantment is employed; it seems simple to you, but it ought to be a great treasure. In this box there is a little amber ball; if you always carry it with you, not only will you be protected from everything that anyone might attempt against your life, but a year of its possession will give you the art of enchantment. The faculties of the body are attached to the box, and those of the soul to the amber ball. If you lose the ball separately from the box, those who possess it will have total power over your soul, but without your being able to die, since they will only have half the charm; it is the same with regard to the box, if you lose it. So, conserve this precious treasure that my amity is leaving you.

"I shall quit you soon; it is necessary that Zineby and I arrive at the palace today, in order not to give any suspicion of your flight. I shall tell your women that I have permitted you to spend a few days alone with your friend in the palace of pleasures. In a short while we will come to find you again, but don't wait for me to conclude your marriage; it's necessary that it takes place tomorrow, in order to take all hope away from Prince Jealous. If he tries to break knots respected by the gods, his crime will render him weaker and give us arms against him.

We entered port as she finished speaking. The fay's slave genii had brought the principal noblemen of the court to meet us, with the chiefs of the army and the people, followed by an innumerable cried of inhabitants. They rendered homage to their prince and caused to burst forth, in a thousand cries of joy, the pleasure they felt in rediscovering in him their legitimate king.

We were taken to the palace; there, in the presence of the fay, Sedy Assan explained his wishes to them and ordered that everything be prepared for the celebration of the wedding the following day. Having embraced us both, Beneficent assured the chiefs of the realm of her protection.

As I was about to see her depart, a black presentiment troubled me; I yielded to affliction, and my adieux would not have let the fay depart if she had not been taken from my arms. The prince, penetrated by my dolor, tried to calm it with the hope of son seeing her again. I was taken to my apartment, and the women who were to serve me regarded me from that moment on as their queen.

The fay had left several genii with us; two of them in particular were intended to watch over our conservation; the one given to the prince was Norghean and mine was Kalem.

The next day, when everything was ready for the ceremony, I went with the prince to the throne room, which is preceded by the twelve that you have traversed. It was superbly ornamented; all the noblemen of the realm accompanied us, magnificently dressed.

Sedy Assan saw with delight the happy moment arriving that would join my destiny with his, and enjoyed the praises that were given to my feeble beauty. The usual ceremonies had commenced when the daylight was sudden obscured, thunder rumbled and lightning penetrated the chamber; it seemed to us that everything was on fire, and a man was seen to enter, who, approaching us precipitately, cried: "Stop! Stop, traitors! Death alone must unite you!"

Gods, what was my fear when I recognized the jealous Prince Kiribanou! I tried to flee, but my strength failed me; my women, who saw me pale and trembling, hastened to relieve me. Alas, their cares were to be fatal! My ivory box fell from my bosom and opened as it fell, Kiribanou seized it.

In spite of my weakness, perceiving the amber ball on the floor, which had fallen out of it, I picked it up and my first movement was to swallow it. Meanwhile, the cruel prince threw a liquid in my face and pronounced the words: "Change form and become marble."

Immediately, my body was metamorphosed, as you have seen, into marble of three colors. I felt myself transported by a whirlwind of flame and smoke, and found myself placed on a pedestal in a place that was unknown to me; it was the sad cypress wood in which you spoke to me.

I shall not pause to depict my anxiety and my dolor; learn what became of Sedy Assan. He had seen Kiribanou seize my box, and the despair that had taken possession of him had prevented him from noticing that the amber ball was not in his power. When he saw me metamorphosed he counted his life for nothing, and threw his little wand at his rival's feet. Then, falling upon him, sword in hand, he said: "Is it necessary to excite you to take my life?"

Prince Jealous, who was invulnerable, without replying, touched his forehead with a ring he had on his finger; instantly, the ground opened up and swallowed him.

At those words, Abdelazis interrupted her discourse in order to shed tears for the unfortunate Sedy Assan. "What woes, my dear Prince, have you not suffered since that time? Your death would have been too mild then for the cruel Kiribanou; whatever hope I have of seeing you again, you are alas, still suffering!"

Then she wiped away her tears and continued.

It is necessary to tell you how far the barbarian pushed his rage. He touched the throne with his ring, pronouncing the same words again. At the same instant, this palace changed, and the inhabitants of the realm were all metamorphosed into various sorts of insects and animals.

I had not seen the end of that tragic adventure. I did not know where I was and I imagined that I had been transported to another realm. Can you imagine, Boca, the horror of my situation? Less occupied with my deplorable fate than that of my dear prince, I did not know whether, more fortunate than me, he had conserved Beneficent's present; as he had witnessed my misfortune, and I knew his amour, I could not doubt his despair.

I did not hope to see my protectress again; I had lost Zineby forever; and to complete my disgrace, it was not in my power to give myself death. In vain I summoned it to my aid, but cruelly, it was deaf to my voice.

Meanwhile, Beneficent, on returning to the Isle of Ebony, had learned that Envious and Kiribanou had arrived a moment after our flight, had searched for us everywhere, and had both retired precipitately with furious and menacing expressions. Soon, the genii Norghean and Kalem presented themselves before her; they told her about our misfortune, and how destiny had prevailed over their care.

The fay protectress immediately went to gather a few of her friends, and they all promised to second her in opposing their power to the fury of my enemies. The Book of Destinies was consulted, and Beneficent, informed of the resources that still remained to her, left Zineby with one of her fays and came to see me in order to console me.

She sympathized with me and informed me of what I have just told you, adding that Prince Jealous, in order to render Sedy Assan's fate more frightful, had imprisoned him in a cavern excavated under the pedestal on which I was posed; that he had attached him by an invisible force to a pyre, and, insulting his misfortune, he had approached him, holding a blazing torch in his hand, and said: "This funeral torch will take the place of the nuptial torch for you; it alone can set light to your pyre. It will never go out, and when you are weary of suffering, if you have strength enough to kill yourself, set fire to it. I leave you that resource. Then he placed the fatal torch in a corner of the cavern and disappeared.

"The unfortunate Sedy Assan," she continued, "has made futile efforts since then to escape from his place and make use of the only resource that can terminate his unfortunate destiny, but supernatural bonds render his strength impotent and his desires superfluous. He hears your plaints, but, unaware that you still conserve a residuum of life, he takes them for those of your moaning shade, reproaching him for the days that are prolonged against his will. Retain, then, Princess, the sighs that augment his despair. I have already told you that hope still remains. Sedy Assan has not lost his life. Zineby is safe; I have saved her from Kiribanou.

"What I have read in the future has informed me that Envious, pressed by her nephew, has given him her power; that prince, yielding to his range, has used it like a fury, allowing himself to be carried away by the passion that gives him, sparing nothing to satisfy his vengeance and not seeing that blindness and error are making him take unreliable routes for the execution of his projects. I shall employ everything to profit from his furious imprudence. I foresee difficulties in that, but, my dear Abdelazis, oppressed innocence has powerful resources against crime. I do not reproach you for the weakness that has attracted you to such great misfortunes; render yourself worthy by your courage of the care that I will take to terminate them."

She quit me then, and I did not see her again for a month.

After that time, I saw her arrive with my dear Zineby. "I have brought you a virtuous and tender friend," the fay said to me, "who wants absolutely to share your misfortune and to expose herself for your sake to frightful perils."

"Oh, Madame," said Zineby, "can I see my princess in this disastrous state without offering her my help, at the expense of my life?"

I wanted to know what that speech signified, and Beneficent spoke. "I was not mistaken," she told me, "when I thought that the cruel Kiribanou's charm would be difficult to destroy, but I was also right to believe that his blindness might serve us. He cannot do anything beyond what he has done; his precipitation to punish his rival caused him to neglect to seize the little wand that Sedy Assan threw at his feet by virtue of a generous despair. The attentive Norghean picked it up and came to return it to me. That mistake might cost Kiribanou dear.

"But that is not all; it is necessary to recover the box that is in his power. Kalem has taken charge of that; I have every hope. He is adroit and has a perfect subtlety. What appears to me very difficult of execution is that bizarre destiny determines that this adventure can only be terminated by a foreigner of obscure birth, but born naturally virtuous, simple, discreet, courageous, submissive and compassionate. It is also necessary that the same man can make a box similar to the one that Kiribanou stole from you, which resembles it perfectly, and that Kalem can make the exchange without the prince perceiving it. It is necessary that the little wand be put in his hands in order to be able to disenchant Sedy Assan and his entire realm, and that he undertake the voyage voluntarily, however long it might be. It is only permitted to me to give birth in him to the desire, and to give him certain limited aid. Prince Jealous does not have a power more extensive than mine to prevent him from succeeding. He can only frighten him and tempt his virtue. But if he is firm, exact and courageous, nothing will be capable of resisting him.

"Kiribanou, who knows that a stranger can destroy his enchantments has changed the greatest city in this realm into a forest and has left several genii there to guard it and to oppose by their malign artifices all those who try to help you. Supposing that he is courageous enough to surmount all those obstacles, it is still necessary for him to be guided here; the road that reads here is frightful. I cannot destroy its horror, nor guide him along that route myself; it's necessary that there is one person in the world who loves you enough to wait for your liberator near this terrible place in order to conduct him, and to risk the death by which he is threatened.

"Your entire court knows what I have just told you; they feel sorry for you, but few want to risk their lives. The king and the queen were the only ones who disputed it with Zineby, but her pleas and my advice made them yield the honor of that heroic action to her. I shall protect her in that enterprise as much as I can; let us leave the rest to the gods,"

When the fay had stopped talking, I opposed Zineby's design; I implored Beneficent to spare me the dolor of her loss, preferring the state I was in to the despair that would follow it; but this tender friend listened impatiently to my speech, burning with impatience to be taken to the place marked for her sacrifice. For two days

I was agitated by a cruel anxiety; Beneficent came to calm me and to tell me that Zineby was still alive; that she had employed a powerful charm to protect her from the efforts that Kiribanou's genii were making to doom her; and that if her zeal did not make her cross the bounds of a road that was prescribed to her, she had nothing to fear, but that one step beyond it would end her days.

"Two men," she added, "attracted by my promises, are on their way here; hope, Princess, and give a truce to your sighs."

Alas, they were only suspended for a short time. I knew that one of them, after having endured a few days of fatigue, had renounced his enterprise, and that the other had succumbed to the first proof and had been metamorphosed in the forest into a ferocious beast. Many others have had the same fate, and for two years, Boca, I learned almost every day that all those in whom Beneficent had inspired the desire to come here had not had the strength to overcome slight obstacles, and that, in succumbing to them, they had given the seductive genii the power to metamorphose them into vile animals. It was those unfortunates who frightened you so much with their cries in the obscure passage into which Zineby led you. You doubtless expected soon to become their prey, but those frightful howls were only plaints and regrets they were giving to the imminent misfortune that threatened you.

At the end of the second year, my protectress came to tell me that she had found in you, Boca, a man capable of fulfilling her designs; that the candor of your mores and the skill of your workmanship seconded her hopes.

"Never," she said, "has anyone turned ivory better than that man does. All the boxes I have had until now have been defective by comparison with those Boca makes. I've charged the genius Norghean to obtain one, in his own fashion. He has just brought me the last one; it's so similar to the one that Kiribanou is keeping from us that I could mistake it myself.

At this point Boca interrupted the princess for the first time, uttering a profound sigh.

"Alas, Madame," he said, "if I had known then the utility of that box, and to what I had destined it, I would not have experienced the profound displeasure that I felt, and would have come sooner to serve you with a good heart."

"I have no doubt of it," replied Abdelazis, "but Boca, it was not permitted to the fay Beneficent to inform you; your consent and hazard had to act in association with her cause. Norghean, in order to engage you to perfect your work, paid you an excessive price...."

"Good," said Boca. "You don't know, then, Princess, that all that money vanished, and that instead of finding the piastres where I had stored them preciously, nothing came out of my coffers but flies, ants and other animals?"

"I know that," she replied, smiling, "but Boca, when one wants to know a man, it is necessary to see him in adversity. That first proof made us believe that you were capable of sustaining the others. Confess that the treasure that the old man offered to share with you in the forest would have tempted you if you had not already reflected on the fragility of perishable wealth. The insects that you found in place of your money were inhabitants of this realm, who, knowing that you might contribute to my deliverance, wanted to prove their zeal to me. If hazard had enabled you to interrogate them, they would have responded, as I did, and engaged you to undertake the voyage; that was the sole fashion of speech permitted to them. You did not do it, and her cares were futile."

"What, Madame!" said Boca. "That beautiful bird, and that frightful spider would have spoken to me?"

"Yes," she said, "the bird would have spoken to you, but I don't know whether the spider would have done; it was occupied with another concern."

Gradually, Boca, you're engaging me in a greater detail; you want to know everything. It's necessary, then, that you know that Kiribanou, in metamorphosing the subjects of his empire, added to their torture that of being forced to follow the natural instinct of the species into which they had been transformed, an instinct that he had chosen directly opposed to their character.

Philosophers became butterflies; men of letters, politicians and magistrates were changed into cockchafers. The assiduous courtier, better treated than the others, conserved by the beauty of his plumage the former marks of his adornment, but, fleeing slavery, he became an inhabitant of the air, and, flying from branch to branch, he sang the praises of a forced liberty of which he did not know the price.

Prodigal women became ants, nonchalant and avaricious ones were constrained to work or others in the form of honey-bees. Old prudes in appearance and coquettes in fact, whose entire care was to repair with artistry and in secret the outrages that time was inflicting on their beauty, saw themselves dolorously transformed into monstrous spiders displaying an unworthy toil in daylight and only exciting horror and fear by their presence.

The one that pursued the bird in your bedroom had once loved him; he was a man of distinguished merit who had only had scorn for her; seeking to avenge herself for a long time, she took the opportunity to place herself in one of your coffers with the others, under the pretext of serving me. You saw how she pursued and stung the poor bird; indignant at that action, Norghean punished her, but her death did not prevent the poor nobleman from suffering cruelly and having lost his life in Beneficent's service; for, Boca, the poisoned inclinations of a prudish and aged coquette are very dangerous.

Seeing that you had become accustomed to those prodigies, the fay enabled you to find the little wand, and in order to engage you to guard it preciously, she attached to it the gift of producing four reals every day when it was in your pocket. She dictated the oracle, you departed and I knew every day by way of my protectress what was happening to you on the way.

I learned, when you were in Java, how she engaged you to board the little vessel that brought you here; that, guided and served by the most jealous subjects of Sedy Assan, her genius Norghean preserved you from several dangers by combating hose of Prince Jealous; and that eventually, courageous, firm and virtuous, you had overcome the three obstacles of the forest; but I can only think about the fourth while shivering again.

You were about to perish, my dear Zineby (She embraced her as she spoke) when, at the sight of Boca, transported by joy and full of confidence, you ran to met him, crossing the prescribed limits and forgetting the danger. Alas, generous stranger, if your courage and compassion had not hastened your steps, she would have lost her life. The virtue of the little wand you were crying immobilized Prince Jealous's malevolent genii.

She guided you, and at the moment when you fell, unconscious, Norghean transported you into the garden where you remained asleep all night. Beneficent and Zineby spent it with me, and we flattered ourselves with an imminent success. Kalem confirmed our hope and brought the fay the ivory box that he had just stolen from Kiribanou, after having replaced it with yours. The genius was charged with extracting you from your torpor at daybreak, and Beneficent instructed me as to what I had to order you to do, if, by chance, our questions permitted me to speak; and above all, to instruct you not to close the doors of the palace, certain that they would not open again, that you would perish therein and that the little wand would be in the power of our enemy.

"You know the rest, until the moment when you quit me to go to the palace; you have seen the violent situation I was in, and how Kalem received in the box the little amber ball that emerged from my mouth; the genius immediately put it in the hands of the fay, who had remained invisible beside me, and Norghean bought Zineby back to us.

Abdelazis was still speaking when Norghean and Kalem came in and addressed Boca. "Come immediately," they said. "All is lost if you delay. Kiribanou has perceived the deceit that has been perpetrated, and the unfortunate Sedy Assan is about to perish if you do not help him. The barbarian has ordered one of his genii to go and set light to his pyre. Go and find the fay, who is waiting for you near the pedestal. Don't follow us, Princess. Beneficent wants you to remain with Zineby."

Boca went with them, and as soon as he had joined the fay, she assured him that nothing disastrous would happen to him.

"But," she added, "as soon as my genii have taken you down into the cave under this pedestal, let nothing frighten you. Go immediately to take the blazing torch that you will see there. Don't listen to what Sedy Assan says, and without replying to him, shake the torch twice. Two large flaming embers will fall from it. Step on them boldly and crush them. Then throw the torch on the pyre."

After that instruction she commanded him to strike the pedestal with his wand. It broke, the ground opened, and Boca was transported to the floor of the cave.

By the light of the deadly torch he saw the unfortunate prince imploring him insistently to bring it to him, but without paying him any heed, he did exactly what had been prescribed to him.

Scarcely had he crushed the embers and thrown the torch on to Sedy Assan's pyre than the earth trembled, frightful cries were heard, and the pyre caught fire instantly and was consumed.

Boca deplored the fate of the prince and, believing that he had just perished, he was reproaching himself for having been the cause of it when he found himself in the garden, where Sedy Assan had already preceded him, with the assistance of Norghean.

The prince was at the feet of the fay; the charm had been destroyed at the moment when Boca had stamped on the embers.

They went to find the princess; her joy was describable.

"You have nothing more to fear," the fay said to them. "Live in security, fortunate lovers; your enemies have just perished; all their malice resided in that torch and their lives were attached to the ardent embers that Boca has just crushed. Thus perish, in the end, the unjust fays whose great number of crimes causes them to lose their immortality.

"Everything here is resuming its ordinary form. Receive from me, both of you, the art of enchantment. I know you well enough not to fear that you might abuse it. You are about to have your wishes fulfilled; let a just moderation guide you, and let the memory of your past misfortunes defend you from the blindness into which an excess of good fortune often causes people to fall. Let Zineby choose in this court a husband worthy of her heart: I shall not make her any gifts, in order not to deprive you, Abdelazis, of the pleasure you will have in rendering her happy.

"Let us see what I can do for you, Boca," she said, turning toward him. "It is only just to lavish the greatest benefits on those who have rendered us such important services; set no limits on our gratitude. Speak; you have only to ask."

"Madame," relied Boca, "I heard the princess say that the animals that frightened me with their cries in the forest were unfortunates who, like me, tried to help her. Please disenchant those poor folk and send them back to their homelands. Perhaps they have families or relatives who cannot subsist without them, and who are not complicit in their faults. In any case, Madame, I confess to you that I don't know why I didn't succumb, like them; doubtless you have supported me with a greater assistance."

"I'm glad to see, Boca," the fay said, "that your virtue is pure enough to mistake itself. My justice has anticipated your wish; those men have already resumed their original forms; but it's very little to return them to their homelands. My treasures are open to you; make them all presents, which satisfy your generous heart, and for yourself, choose the country in which you want to enjoy the fortune that I am preparing for you."

Then Boca turned to Abdelazis and Sedy Assan. "If the king will be kind enough," he said, "to let me remain in this city, I shall spend the rest of my days here. I have a few relatives and friends; I shall share your benefits with them, and this realm will take the place of my homeland. But please, Madame, don't give me too much wealth; it seems to me that I'd be less happy. Permit me to occupy myself turning ivory again; I owe too much to that petty talent not to make it my greatest pleasure,"

Everyone admired Boca's moderation; everything that he requested was granted to him.

Abdelazis and Sedy Assan were married with pomp and magnificence. The King and Queen of the Isle of Ebony witnessed their daughter's wedding, and Zineby, heaped with wealth and honors, received a husband from the hands of Abdelazis not long afterwards.

Boca was given a small apartment in the palace. The candor of his mores, his disinterest, his humanity and his frankness earned him the love and honor of everyone; which proves that virtue, in order to be respected, has no need to borrow the splendor of riches or grandeurs.

CLASSIC FRENCH FANTASY

Honoré de Balzac. *The Last Fay*
Gabrielle-Suzanne Barbot de Villeneuve. *The Naiads   Beauty and The Beast*
Chevalier de Béthune. *The World of Mercury*
Jean Carrère. *The End of Atlantis*
Charlotte-Rose Caumont de La Force. *The Land of Delights*
Félicien Champsaur. *Pharaoh's Wife*
Jacques Collin de Plancy. *Voyage to the Center of the Earth*
Gaston Danville. *The Perfume of Lust*
Comtesse D.L. *The Tyranny of the Fays Abolished*
Paul Féval. *Anne of the Isles*
Charles de Fieux. *Lamékis*
Judith Gautier. *Isoline and the Serpent-Flower*
Nathalie Henneberg. *The Green Gods*
Gustave Kahn. *The Tale of Gold and Silence*
Edmond Haraucourrt. *Dieudonat*
Marie-Jeanne L'Héritier de Villandon. *The Robe of Sincerity*
André Lichtenberger. *The Centaurs; The Children of the Crab*
J-M. & Randy Lofficier. *The French Fantasy Treasury 1-3*
Charles Lomon & P.-B. Gheuzi. *The Last Days of Atlantis*
Maurice Magre. *The Marvelous Story of Claire d'Amour; The Call of the Beast; Priscilla of Alexandria; The Angel of Lust; The Mystery of the Tiger; The Poison of Goa; Lucifer; The Blood of Toulouse; The Albigensian Treasure; Jean de Fodoas; Melusine; The Brothers of the Virgin Gold*
Marie-Madeleine de Lubert. *Princess Camion.*
Camille Mauclair. *The Virgin Orient*
Hippolyte Mettais. *Paris Before the Deluge*
Victor-Emile Michelet. *Superhuman Tales*
Henriette-Julie de Murat. *The Palace of Vengeance*
Charles Nodier. *Trilby   The Crumb Fairy*
Edgar Quinet. *The Enchanter Merlin*

Le bruit qu'ils firent en marchant
la tira de sa reverie.

www.ingramcontent.com/pod-product-compliance
Lightning Source LLC
Chambersburg PA
CBHW030330020726
47493CB00004B/1215